QU

Susan Mann grew up in Durban, South Africa
before relocating to Cape Town, where she now
lives. She has worked in the media and studied
and taught at the University of Cape Town.

ALSO BY SUSAN MANN

One Tongue Singing

SUSAN MANN

Quarter Tones

VINTAGE BOOKS
London

Published by Vintage 2007

2 4 6 8 10 9 7 5 3 1

Copyright © Susan Mann 2007

Susan Mann has asserted her right under the Copyright, Designs and
Patents Act 1988 to be identified as the authors of this work

First published in Great Britain in 2007 by
Harvill Secker
Random House, 20 Vauxhall Bridge Road,
London SW1V 2SA

www.vintage-books.co.uk

Addresses for companies within The Random House Group Limited
can be found at: www.randomhouse.co.uk/offices.htm

The Random House Group Limited Reg. No. 954009

A CIP catalogue record for this book
is available from the British Library

ISBN 9780099502678

The Random House Group Limited makes every effort to ensure that
the papers used in its books are made from trees that have been
legally sourced from well-managed and credibly certified forests.
Our paper procurement policy can be found at:
www.rbooks.co.uk/environment

Printed in the UK by CPI Bookmarque, Croydon, CR0 4TD

For Carol and Niall Mann

hear me please, I said –
this, my home address, is almost a smudge
a bloody smudge
almost like nothing
I squint to see it

> – Mongane Wally Serote

The same loneliness that closes us
opens us again.

> – Anne Michaels

AGAIN AT NIGHT the field of burning flowers. Burning in the yellow glare of noon, just burning, no smoke, never dying. Till the image singes the membrane between sleep and non-sleep. She does not open her eyes, does not move a muscle. Hoping that if she lies still enough, curled like a shell, she might float in this fluid between dark and light, yesterday and today, sea and earth. *Between.* Waiting. Till she hears again the voices she carries in her skin. Before the day breaks open and spills into what people call *the real world*.

ONE

IT WAS WINTER when she finally went back, just too late. The hired car bounced and lurched along the road, turning up from the beach, towards the mountain, now and again skidding through a puddle then a pothole, revving too high. In the rainlight of that late afternoon, the driveway uncurled like a serpent, and ahead the garden, his garden, grew wild. Weeds waist-high between the fynbos. Lavender straggling and woody. You must have been ill for a long time, she thought. Even the bridge over the river was broken on one side, and somewhere behind it all hunched the cottage she still called home.

The old man had been asking for her – for his daughter, Ana Luisa – for days, they said. Why didn't you let me know? she wanted to ask. I would have come earlier. Why didn't you tell me? But instead she nodded, took the keys and stuffed them into her bag, even mumbled thank you.

Sam. A part of her would forever see him flinging open the stable doors, peeling the gardening gloves from his square fingers, and walking towards her with white hair, stocky frame and slightly bow-legged gait. There would be light in the kitchen, smoke from the chimney, a house with a heartbeat. Not this little shack shrouded in a net of rain, like some frail hermit hiding from the world.

It was late August, the winter after the fires of 2000. For days the runaway flames roared and crackled right across the mountain, leaping like rabid dogs across streets and through the valleys, devouring mile after mile of vegetation. He only told her about it a week later. How on the first day – that dark afternoon in January, when the sun filled with blood, and later spat residues of ash down on the city – people had fled from their offices, trying to get home, gripping their steering wheels with white knuckles and hooting, imagining what might happen to their animals, their homes, if they did not get back in time to hose down their borders, their roofs. It was quite something, he said. How people had fought for their homes for days without sleeping, their eyes parched and blazing. How helicopters carrying water had chugged and whirred till dusk and firefighters had kept going, night after night. The ground was scorched. Trees like charred skeletons. The small animals – tortoises, porcupines, snakes – had not made it, he found their burnt shells and bits of skin every so often on the mountain. He was grateful for his own firebreak, he said. And so was the garden. Even so, he had watered the thatch on the hour just in case.

She shuddered as she drove over Ou Kaapse Weg twisting through the fold of mountains. The road she knew so well – flanked by Silvermine Nature Reserve on both sides, curling round and down towards the sea – felt alien. Like driving over the moon. White. Sterile. All that remained of the succulent vegetation, the fynbos, the vygies, was ash and dust. Seven months later and she could smell it even with the windows closed. She turned right into Silvermine Road and fumbled around the dashboard for the lights.

She parked the car in front of the back door, switching

off the rainwipers, but leaving the car idling and head-lamps on. Not that it was too dark to see – to find the key or the cylinder for the gas – but because there was some comfort in the rhythm of the engine and the light. Only once she had let herself into the kitchen, and inhaled its stale familiarity, did she dart back to the vehicle, switch off the ignition and remove the two items she had brought with her from the boot: a small leather bag carrying her clothes, and a black flute case. With a swing she hoisted her luggage onto the heavy table in the centre of the room. Still holding the handle of the flute case, she started making her way into the rest of the cottage. Her footfall, tap, tap, tap on the quarry tiles, and somewhere in the silence, the churn of the sea.

The central living area was a pale replica of what she remembered. The arthritic chairs, wooden arms curled inward, the curtains now threadbare, some portraits, a sketch of her mother, in one corner the gramophone, in the other his harpsichord. From where she stood, she could see the dust on the wooden staircase up to the two bedrooms. Instinctively, she lifted the flute case up to her chest and hugged it.

It had once been a sweet factory. Still had some of the old industrial fittings, heavy counters on quarry-tiled floors, metal lamps and overhead fans, a long loft, his workshop, above the kitchen, and two bedrooms on the other side. The original owner of the property, something of a recluse, had lived next door. At the time he believed it possible to bring business to himself, instead of fighting traffic into Cape Town every day. But as the confectionery grew increasingly successful and he was forced to hire more and more staff, his privacy felt under siege. Eventually he moved the business to an industrial area and sold the company. A few years later, with no further use for it, he sold the cottage to a young Irishman and his nervous wife. For a song, her father told someone. He'd bought it for a song.

Which one? she asks. She can't be more than seven or eight.

Which what, dear? he replies.

Which song? Was it an *aria*? She knows the word from music lessons.

No, not an aria, he replies. That would be too expensive. More like, more like an everyday song.

Like *I'll be your long-haired lover from Liverpool*? She's heard it on the radio. She likes it. Almost as much as *Tie a Yellow Ribbon*.

Yes, dear, I suppose so, he says. He looks a bit surprised. More like that.

Her father was thirty when he bought the property for his bride – her age in just a few months' time. For nine years he had been working as a luthier, restoring and making stringed instruments in a small alley off Long Street in the city. He had rented an office on the second floor, above the jewellery shop, the jewellery shop where he'd met her mother. When Ana was a little girl, he would take her there to see it, now and again. At the time she thought he did it to give them an outing, to get them out of the house. Later she understood that this was part of his endless grieving, the going back and retracing every step that had led to his finding, then losing, the woman he married.

The woman was the daughter of the watchmaker, a Portuguese man who had married a South African woman and worked for the jeweller's beneath Sam's office for most of his life. She was only eighteen, your mother, he reminded her. A sylph of a woman,

6

a *suggestion*, slipping in and out of the store like sunlight.

She stopped in front of her mother's portrait. A swirl of pastel lines showed a narrow face. As a child she'd spent hours staring at the drawing, willing it to live. When she was six, her father once caught her trying to pull the frame apart, stopped her just in time. She never told him why; that all she wanted was to make the faded lines a little darker. To access something – a memory perhaps, a story. To concretise the ghost. A short while later, there had been the episode with the broken glass. No trace of that now, the glass had been replaced. Although she suspected the woman in the drawing had never quite forgiven her.

Never mind, she whispered to the portrait. Don't look so anxious. Tomorrow I'll start to clean, all right?

After her father left the office off Long Street, it was used as a storage room, so did not much resemble how it had been, he said. Still, he wanted to show it to her. She remembered it had a small window with black panes that overlooked a passageway. Remembered how he moved between the boxes, explaining how he'd divided the room in two; the front half for customers and work, the back, with the little enamel basin and old brass taps, for his mattress and gramophone. His treasured collection of vinyl records. Poulenc, Hindemith, Beethoven.

She loved the flute, your mother, he often said. How she loved the flute.

He examined the door, growing suddenly alive when he saw the two holes that showed where his name plate had once been screwed in.

It read *Samuel Delaney: Luthier*, he told her, marvelling at the block of wood. Funny isn't it, he muttered, that a door, of all things, should continue to be.

Not so funny, Sam, she later wished she could reply. A door still has possibilities.

After the wedding, he moved his workshop from Long Street back home to Noordhoek. She could see it from where she was standing, the loft; rows of shelves stacked with wooden planes and tools. A square of light broke through the window, through veins of dirt and dust. Stringed instruments were his speciality – violins, guitars, even mandolins. But he tinkered with others too. Harpsichords. Pianos. His favourite harpsichord was one he had made himself from a kit that came in an enormous box, by ship from England. They had tied it to the roof of the old red Mercedes with orange string and driven very slowly from the harbour, very slowly, with her praying all the way that it wouldn't fall off.

Be-ware of the hum-ps, she reads slowly on a sign-board, as they draw closer to home. What's a hump, Sam?

A hump? You don't know about humps?

No. What's a hump?

It's short for heffalump, dear. One must be careful in these parts.

What do they look like? she wants to know.

Just normal, he says. Like a normal giant, you know. Nothing special.

Hmm, she says. I think you're telling fibs.

Me? he says, making his eyes round.

Yes.

She leans forward, as close to his face as she could reach with the seatbelt on. Sam . . . look me in the eye and tell me again without smiling.

But I'm driving, dear. With a replica of a seventeenth-century harpsichord on the roof of the car.

Fibs, she nods to herself, settling back into the seat. I can tell.

And how is that, then? He keeps his eyes big.

Because. Because a giant *is* special.

Ah, quite right, dear. Quite right.

He will need to have the inside lid painted, he explains, changing the subject. The Italians decorated their instruments, you see.

She offers to help, she has her paints in her bedroom, but he says that it is not the job for someone who is only nine. Maybe when she turns ten.

The harpsichord takes three months to make. Every day after school she sits alongside him in her school uniform, the oversized brown tunic and stiff hat, and watches, knocking him now and then with the rim of the hat, and handing him tools as he asks for them. He explains each part of the exercise, as he works.

The notes are made from boxwood, Ana, he says. See? And the black notes out of stained pear.

Will it have jumping jacks? she wants to know.

She knows all about jumping jacks from the spinet he had resurrected the year before.

And what about cow-bone studs?

She has a special fascination for the spinet's cow-bone studs. Her father had turned each one, each one made from the bones of cows, each one smaller than a jelly tot, about fifty in all, then stuck them into the harpsichord to hold the wood together.

The spinet was really something, he said. She remembers the plectrums that he made for it, from the spines of seagull feathers that they found on Noordhoek Beach. They would comb the beach for hours with a

Pick 'n Pay packet pretending they were trackers, working out all the imprints on the beach. From footprints (grown-ups' or children's) to paw-prints (big dog or small) to hoof-prints, shell-prints or the daisy trail left by the sandpipers. Then back at the cottage she would watch, as he honed a small piece of quill, the size of a nail clipping, or a new moon, into a tiny point, no bigger than a pinhead.

It's the quills that make the plucking sound, Ana, he taught her. Listen.

And he would play songs that made her think of banjos and guitars.

And there it was, still in the living room, in the corner. She looked around and shook her head. The chairs all seemed to face the wrong way, the table leg was broken, lace curtains hung limp and yellowed. A matching tablecloth cloaked a table on which some photographs huddled, pictures of herself as a little girl smiling fatly into the camera, later at eleven or twelve, with the flute. She looked down at the black case she was still holding, before placing it on the sofa and returning to the faded picture, the white of the eyes of a child willing that musical instrument to sing, fingers birdlike. Then with both hands she lifted towards her a colour shot of herself and Michael on the ferry at Dover, en route to Paris for their honeymoon. Smiling, smiling. *My happy daughter*, her father must have thought.

She turned to the light, half expecting him to walk through the door. Then imagined him in his chair by the window, doing the crossword, his spectacles falling halfway down his nose. She picked up the flute case again, and went back to the kitchen, stopping to run her hand over the interleading yellowwood door. She remembered driving with him to buy the yellowwood tree. Standing alongside him as he chopped it, *careful Ana, mind your face*, then watching him planing it by hand. Watching the nails hammered in.

That's where *dead as a doornail* comes from, he says, banging another one in and flattening it on the other side.

What about swinging a cat, she wants to know. *Not enough room to swing a cat.* Where does that come from?

Hmm? he mumbles, concentrating, a nail between his teeth.

I hate that one, she says, raising her voice in case he hits another nail. The one about swinging a cat.

She still hated it. Along with all the other animal metaphors. *Kill two birds with one stone. Easy as clubbing seals. Keep your eye on the fox.* She put her flute on the kitchen table. In the drawer she found some matches and a packet of candles.

Let me light one for you, she said, half believing he would walk through the door. As the flame ignited, she heard a knock. She swung round to face a man of indeterminate age standing under a black umbrella in the doorframe, slightly stooped, like a bird of prey.

Sorry, didn't mean to frighten you, he said. I heard you were coming, I'm Franz van der Veer, I live next door. I wanted to say how sorry I am . . . your father . . . and bring you some provisions.

He held out his hand over the closed half of the stable door. She stared at it, blew out the match, then leaned forward and shook it.

Ana, she said, feeling her hand disappear like a glove into his grip.

With a nod, he lifted a basket over the bottom of the stable door. You must be very tired.

Thank you, she said.

Not at all, he replied, staring at her. Tell me, was there a funeral?

No, she said. No funeral. He was cremated before I got here.

I never knew he was ill, he said. But then, once it's in the lymph, ja, it's very quick, isn't it. How long are you planning to stay?

I don't know, she said. Till I know what to do next.

Her eyes narrowed as she watched his outline from the window after bolting the door behind him. A tall, slightly bent angular man striding through the mud and grass in the rain. The son of the recluse who owned the sweet factory, she figured. As a child she never knew what happened in the big house next door. She vaguely remembered rumours. A family feud between brothers. Someone had died. Someone had left. But a stone wall and a line of plane trees had divided the two properties, and she was never quite tall enough to see over them. She looked at the basket, lifted the corner of the red and white tea towel covering it: a ham, a selection of cheeses, a seed loaf, some snoek pâté and a bottle of red wine, *Goats Do Roam*. She covered it again. Maybe later.

Of course there was no funeral. Who would have attended? And anyway, her father hated funerals. Said the organs were often out of tune, people's eardrums too addled with grief and wanting the whole damn thing over with as soon as possible, to care about false strains.

In the bathroom she opened the taps to check the temperature, before running a deep bath. As the water first gurgled and sputtered then gushed into the old enamel tub, she stared at her reflection in the mirror pocked with rust. You've lost too much weight, she knew her father would have said if he were to see this face, all eyes and angles. And the protruding hip bones, with no flesh to protect them, often bruised, certainly not child-bearing. She suddenly thought of something and counted on her fingers. Ten. It had been ten months since she'd bled, and still no sign of it. Then suddenly, with the water still filling the bath she rummaged in the cabinet and found a pair of scissors. Before she knew it, she had released the ponytail from its tired elastic band, and, pulling the brown hair down with one hand, prised open the pair of scissors, sawing off every strand at the neck.

TWO

IT WAS THE birds that woke her. Starlings. Either that or the silence, she couldn't decide which. Or perhaps not silence – because the starlings were kicking up quite a racket, and in the distance she could hear the sea – but more absence of city noise: aeroplanes on their flight-paths to and from Heathrow, neighbours banging doors, traffic in the rain. No more London, she thought, squirming deep under the blankets. No more red-brick flat in Barnes, Mr Sinclair next door with his CD player, washing that smells of damp, feet scuffing the pavements rushing for the tube, no more weekly weddings at the Presbyterian church below, no more Michael. No more waiting for him to come home, staring out of the window at the cars moving below in the rain, glow worms crawling through the silver. The street filling, emptying. No more waiting.

Home. Is it a place? A person? A feeling? Could this structure, this collection of bricks and blisters, beams and rust, smell of ozone, possibly be what she'd dreamt of all this time away? Or did it need her father, the penumbra of her mother, to be complete? After the loss had sunk into the walls, would memory be the ghost between, filling the cracks, moving through the air vents, morphing and changing with her own shifts?

For now she could keep her questions. She pulled the

blankets tighter. She didn't have to argue about them with Michael. For him, *home* was a concept, a political theory, his identity linked with its absence of meaning.

The bed creaked like a greeting each time she burrowed into it. Her father had made it for her when she was born, from yellowwood planks he'd bought at an auction in Wynberg. The sheets and blankets were probably the same age. She peered out over them at her bedroom in the daylight, at the thatched roof and poles, the dressing table under the window, the glow of green from the forest in the distance, the kist, a balding rug with some tassels on the wooden floor. The rain had stopped.

She pulled the covers away, slowly, inches at a time, but the cold enveloped her, bit into her uncovered hands and neck. She shrank into her shoulders, drawing the blankets up over her again. Icy after the rain. No heating. But she must get up, get moving, there were things to do. Return the car, get provisions. She thought of her father's bedroom next to hers and sunk back into the warmth. She had closed his door in the dark the previous night, before going to bed. Clutching the blankets under her chin, she stared out through the window at the tips of the trees for some time, the sea in the distance a mass of sapphire silk, crumpled and creased and fraying at the edges. Then, with one decisive shove, she flung them to one side and reached for her jeans, bending and buttoning with small shudders, pulling a sweater over the T-shirt, crumpled and sleep-warm. In the bathroom she took a breath and splashed her face with water, her fingers red, first numb then burning. She caught a glimpse of herself as she shook the water from her face, surprised at the reflection – the suddenly short hair, pale skin. Then she tiptoed downstairs to switch on the kettle.

Treading lightly. It was something she had learned to do from an early age. Since the time when as a child she'd run, jump and slide on the rug in her father's workshop.

Wheeee-kadouff! I exist.

Her father pays no attention to this antic, until one day she runs a little harder and slides right into him.

Oops, she says, skidding to a halt against his shoulder. Sorry, Sam.

The jolt causes him to plane into his thumb, blood spurting out and onto the horsehair of a nearby violin bow. He drops the piece of wood and puts his thumb in his mouth, partly to stop the blood, partly to prevent her from seeing how much it bleeds.

Careful, dear, he says, a little short.

Sorry, Sam, she whispers. Stands there, wide-eyed.

Could you get me a plaster then? he asks.

She tiptoes downstairs to the bathroom. She wants to be invisible. To slip into the cracks in the floorboards. She never wants to be a destructive, noisy child, never a nuisance.

She knows exactly what it cost her father for her to be alive.

And somehow it had stuck. Even in crowds she moved like the wind, like a secret, between people, buildings. Often she had to exhale consciously. Even when a shopkeeper overcharged her, or someone was rude to her, it was she who would apologise. Not because she thought she was in the wrong, but to avoid the smallest threat of being noticed or seen. To avoid the threat, the embarrassment, of leaving a stain on the universe.

It drove Michael crazy.

Jeez, Ana. You give me the screaming heebie-jeebies, creeping up on me like that.

I wasn't creeping up on you.

Well, why is it I never seem to hear you?

Maybe you aren't listening.

She started to notice the different relationship people negotiated with space. Some strode and expanded with every step, monopolising their world at every turn. Others, like herself, negated the space they occupied, cleaning up after themselves, fleeing from their shadows.

In London, Michael bought her a pair of Doc Martens. Hefty black boots that laced halfway up her calves.

Here, for God's sake, wear these. Good strong shoes.

The first time she wore them the ground seemed to reverberate with each footfall. Whether with jeans or skirts, it felt like she was all boots, all *good strong shoes*, with a tread that betrayed her with every step with its clumsy sense of presence. When he was away, she hid the boots in the cupboard. To stop the sound of her own step. To stop it deafening her.

The sun was out in London when she left. A farewell gift, acknowledgement of just over a decade. She warmed her hands around the cup of tea as the vapour rose up over her chin to her mouth. It had been a long time to be away. Not only did she leave her father behind, but possibly much of herself too. They had left South Africa, she and Michael, for Britain in 1989, after he had completed his Political Science degree and received his call-up papers for the army. Over my dead body, he'd said at the time. She agreed with him. The army was a joke as far as they were concerned. *A joke.* He explained to her at length how it used the global fear of communism as a ruse to keep those in power at the helm, to justify division. For Michael to spend any time *in service* was unthinkable. A betrayal of everything he stood for. Within the month they sold his VW Beetle and bought air tickets for Europe.

I'll get a job and you'll play the flute for a real orchestra, he promised. You'll never look back, Ana, he said. You'll never look back because this country's toast.

For the first year they told each other that they were living in exile. It gave them a gravity, and even a certain cachet amongst their peers. They felt that even though they weren't directly involved in The Struggle, they were supporting it far more than if they had remained at home. It also served Michael well in the position he found for himself, as programme manager for an NGO, the Institute for Freedom and Democracy in Africa. IFDA was funded by several Scandinavian countries, and focused on projects aimed at bridging the digital divide. Michael found himself assisting the Director in their Programme for Media and Communications.

Then in 1990, when Mandela was released, the threat of communism suddenly evaporated. With the ANC unbanned, she wanted to return, but Michael initially refused.

It's a circus there, Ana, he said. The crime, the corruption – it will take decades to rectify.

A few years later, at the thought of surfing every weekend, he capitulated temporarily, and applied for a job in South Africa. She held her breath. But when the application was refused on the grounds of affirmative action, he grew more resentful than ever.

Still she wanted to go home, she missed her father, the open spaces, the light. But Michael was adamant. And angry, for some reason. Still longing for a revolution that had seemingly been cancelled. To stop her leaving, he married her.

After the last sip of tea, black because there was no milk, she opened the kitchen door and stepped out into the garden. Raindrops shivered from every blade and branch, the morning sun setting each one alight. With every step she sank into the grass, the sodden earth, twigs and rotting leaves. The air stung her nostrils, numbing her upper lip. She could smell wood smoke; it must be from the house next door. She glanced across in its direction, and noticed that the row of plane trees that had lined the neighbouring property had been felled and the boundary wall had collapsed here and there, like the spine of a skeleton, its bones slowly decaying. Her father would have liked that. It must have reminded him of the Irish countryside, stone walls, centuries old, holding their stories within each stone and pebble, the way we hold memories in our bones. A bird dropped down onto the ground in front of her, whisked a worm from the mud, cocked its head, then sputtered upwards. She heard the sound of a car starting, watched as a shiny 4x4 glided along the brick driveway next door. Suddenly it stopped. With engine still purring, the door opened and a man climbed out and waved at her. When she didn't return the wave, he drove back up the driveway and jumped out of the car. There was something vaguely familiar about the rangy silhouette, slightly stooped, in the crisp suit. She squinted, then realised it was Franz.

Morning, he said. Have a good night there, all alone?

Fine, she nodded. Thanks.

It struck her that *alone* was the last feeling she had experienced.

I'm off to work, can I get you any provisions, perhaps? Something?

He was standing between the car and the open door, his face in the triangle between the two.

No, I don't think so. I need to return the hired car, anyway. Thanks all the same.

Would you like a ride home then, perhaps? I work in the city, off Kloof Street, do you know where that is? I can come home early this afternoon if it would help. He dipped into his jacket pocket and produced a card.

Okay, she said. Yes, I know it. That's kind. Thanks.

Later, she took out the card. Printed in black serif on sheer white, the words *Van der Veer & De Wet: Architects*, his name, contact details and address. She remembered Kloof Street well; it was a continuation of Long, near her father's office, an eclectic mix of houses, blocks of flats, restaurants and shops, here and there balconies leaning over pavements, as if craning to see what went on in the shops below, and near the top, an old park with rusty swings, where vagrants lay passed out in the sun.

Van der Veer & De Wet was housed in a double-storey building alongside one of the old Victorian beauties that graced that part of the city, rezoned for business use. Painted taupe with turquoise and white trim, she could imagine the *renovator's dream* advertisement that might have caught his attention originally. She rang the brass bell, was asked to announce herself through the intercom, then pushed open the glass and chrome door and stepped inside. She was immediately aware of the contrast between his office and his more rustic home. Shafts of light, imposed through skylights and enormous windows cut into the reception room, creating illusions of dimension and depth.

Mr van der Veer, she whispered to the crisp lady holding the telephone.

Take a seat, the lady said.

As she waited, watching the world through the

one-way glass, she noted how things seemed meticu-
lously placed and counterplaced. The rough fabric of
the upholstery with the smooth shiny table tops. The
reception desk, a perfect half circle offset by asym-
metrical lights, the textured carpets, smooth walls, the
muted tones and red rectangular couch. On the chrome
and glass coffee table a single red fluted vase, its
Murano stamp still visible at its base. It felt to her like a
film set.

She did not need to wait long before he appeared.

Ah, he smiled. You're here. Good. I hope you haven't
been waiting long. Just a second while I get my briefcase.

She hoisted herself into the four-wheel drive.

Why didn't you take a taxi from the airport? he said.
Why did you hire a car?

She shrugged. I don't know. I don't really associate
South Africa with taxis. Or at least not in the London
way. I also thought I may need to run around a little.

It's understandable, you've had a big shock, he
offered. Besides, maybe you thought you'd need a
getaway car. Just in case.

My father did have a car. I haven't checked the garage
yet.

The old Merc? he smiled. Can't say I noticed it on the
road much.

He had a motorbike, with a side-car too, she said,
more to herself than to him. But I can't imagine he drove
that much.

Did you go in it?

Occasionally. It was really for my mother. After she
died, he lost interest.

How old were you when she died?

About an hour. She died giving birth to me. I have her
name: Ana Luisa.

They drove up and over Kloof Nek, through the trees and past the turn-off to the cable car. They wound along the edge of the sea, past Clifton Beach, Llandudno and Hout Bay.

Did you grow up next door, then? he asked.

Yes, she said.

Isn't it funny, I practically did too, strange we never met. But then, I suspect I may have a few more years on my clock than you.

She nodded.

I was born in Rhodesia actually. Zimbabwe. The family came to Cape Town, to the house, when I was a boy. Been there ever since, really. Brief stint in residence when I was at university, but then back home. There's quite a bit of space.

Space is something you take for granted, till you move abroad, she said. Do you live with your family?

Both my parents are long gone, so it's just me. And Angelina. Oh, and George and Clementine.

Your children?

Well, yes, I suppose so. Angelina has been the family housekeeper since we came to the Cape. She's getting on now, but still indispensable. Thinks she's my mother. And George and Clementine are my two bulldogs.

No siblings?

A younger brother, Daniel. He doesn't live with me, though. He's somewhere in Africa, making documentaries, saving the world. You?

She shook her head.

They fell into silence on Chapman's Peak Drive, a convoluted stretch that straddled beauty and treachery. On the one side, cliffs fell away into the liquid blue of the Atlantic Ocean. On the other rocks rose high into the sky. Each winter, after the wind and the rains, a boulder of some sort would dislodge itself, and as though pushed by Polyphemus, come careering down, sometimes on a motorist.

Travel at your own risk, said the signpost.

Doom with a view, Michael had called it.

Actually he called the other night. From Zambia, Franz suddenly said. Or Mali, or Benin, or Ethiopia, I can never keep track.

Who? she asked. She was still back a decade, with Michael.

My brother. He offered to come home and fix the wall. You must have seen, it's falling to pieces.

The boundary wall? The stone one? It's lovely.

That's right. But it's more than just a boundary wall, there are some structural reasons for its existence too. Especially a bit higher into the mountain, with banks and all that. I had some engineers look at it. They reckon we must fix it quite soon. I mentioned it to Daniel, and for some reason he's showing some interest in the place for a change. Says he has a gap between films, will come home and do the job.

They broached the final bend. To the stretch of beach that reaches from Noordhoek, where the rocks and dunes meet the water, all the way to Kommetjie. It was as she remembered, only busier. Previously a spray of houses, some holiday homes, salted the landscape. Now mansions squatted on tiny plots of land all over the mountain, like overfed ladies in stilettos. Constantia-by-the-sea.

But the beach was the same; here and there, a wet-suited surfer, like an upright seal, braved the icy waves. The winter sea was up against the relentless north-wester, pushing the tide back on itself, sometimes at more than seventy kilometres an hour, creating mad mohicans of saltspray, while on that beach with sand as fine as kaolin, horses raced the wind.

As far as she remembered, she said, Noordhoek's Long Beach, in spite of its cheery weekend kite-flying and daily dogs, was not friendly.

No, he agreed. Those that love it and walk it know there have been incidents; robbers hiding in the dunes, some in the shipwreck that lies halfway. Rumour had it that one poor sod returned from his walk stark naked, having been relieved of his watch, mobile phone, wallet and clothes.

Then there's the ocean, she added. With its reputation for great white sharks and swimmers who never return.

She did not say that it was here, on Noordhoek Beach, that Michael first popped up out of the sea and into her life. The place of mighty sunsets, he called it. *Look Ana, in every grain of sand a soul.* Nor did she mention that after a storm, she would wait for the rainbows to arc the valley. That once she had run down to follow one and found it ended in Keurboom Road, in a paddock newly covered in cow manure. Or that she once saw it mentioned in a British travel publication as the loneliest place in the world.

THREE

THAT NIGHT SHE unpacked her bag. It had all happened so quickly; the phone call, leaving. Michael was in Paris, where he spent several weeks each month, working with the French branch of IFDA. She had left a message for him on his mobile, even though she knew he would be in meetings all day. By the time he received the call, she would already be on the tube to Heathrow to catch her flight. She considered writing a note and leaving it in the flat on the dining room table, or on the fridge, but changed her mind. Instead, she tried to reach him from her father's house when she arrived, but discovered that the telephone had been disconnected. A part of her felt relieved. It gave her a feasible excuse, a little time to gather up a sentence or two, before she would be required to explain herself.

At the time when she received the call, she had had just under an hour to pack. No suitcase – Michael had that – simply an old leather bag that she'd won in a music competition years ago, before they left for London. The kind too scuffed and worn to use too often, too tatty to give away. She did not mind at all; liked the leather straps and rusty buckles, the creases and the tears that had come with overuse.

Once again it had made an overseas crossing. She pulled off the airline stickers and tags, threw the bag on the bed and opened it. Took out the faded jeans, hiking shoes, a colourful sweater that Michael had bought her from Covent Garden, some T-shirts, underwear, toiletries, a tiny prayer candle in a red plastic container, two worn books: *Cavafy: Selected Poems* and a volume of *Sanskrit Love Poetry,* plus a spiral-bound notebook in which she scribbled her own poetry now and then. For each item she found a place, a shelf with faded paper lining, an old coat hanger. Finally, she unbuckled the separate pouch in the front and took out the scarf in which she had wrapped the tiny cast-iron teapot that Michael had bought her on their honeymoon, from the Chinese tea shop off rue Mouffetard, in Paris. She draped the scarf over the chair in front of the dresser, and placed the teapot on the table next to her bed.

She looked around, digesting the spirit of the house with some of her possessions surrounding her. The new in the old, layers of familiarity. Only the flute had not found a place. She stared at it for some time. Then took a chair, climbed onto it and wedged the hard black case inside the linen cupboard, out of sight. She locked the door, then examined the room from her elevated position.

Yes, it was better. So much better.

She sat on the bed and looked out through the window towards the forest. Somewhere nearby the cry of a rain-bird rose and fell. Strange, she thought, how one could wrestle with a life for over ten years. And then one shock, one phone call, can change it all, catapult you into the past and future, all at once. She had always suspected that she would come back, and that when it happened it would be sudden. Final. And yet she had no answers, no questions. The only thing she knew for certain was that she never wanted to return to London again.

*

She withdrew the small savings Michael always left her when he went away, at the airport; something to live off for a short while. After that, she would need to find a way to survive. Also, she expected there were bills to pay, cremation costs, medicine. These accounts would surely arrive soon; even in the humblest of circumstances, death does not come free.

The next day, she rummaged in the drawers of the desk where her father kept his papers. She pulled out a folder stuffed with electricity and telephone accounts dating back five years. A couple of lapsed telephone reminders had not been opened, near the end. The receipts of some medical bills showed that he had been ill for six months before he died. She shook her head.

Why didn't you tell me, Sam? All alone here, and knowing you were ill, what was the point of that?

She looked up, half expecting a reply. Only the feet of the rain tap-dancing steadily on the thatch.

After a little while, she came across a policy, an annuity fund, to the value of sixty-seven thousand rand and fifty cents. That would be useful. She must contact them somehow. She did not feel like going next door to use the telephone. Franz may think she was taking advantage of his neighbourliness. She found herself pacing across the room, biting her cheek. She would have to reconnect the phone anyway, to overcome this new, subversive need not to be found by Michael. But if Telkom was anything like it was when she left, she could be forced to wait a long time before anything happened.

She climbed over the wall at one of the parts where it was collapsing. This was the first time she had been to the van der Veers'. As a child she had only ever seen the rooftop in the distance. It was a sprawling farmhouse with a deep stoep. A large, complacent home, with hefty whitewashed walls, not the stylised design she might have associated with an architect's choice of residence.

The two bulldogs barked lazily from their kennel, until a black woman in a sky-blue tunic opened the door. With her head wrapped in a navy African print cloth, covering all but a few tufts of grey hair at the temples, it was not easy to tell her age. Her hands flew up to her mouth like a surprised child, causing her to drop the cloth she was carrying.

Haaibo! she said.

Hello. I'm sorry, did I scare you? Ana gave a little laugh.

Eish! said the woman, then laughed too.

I'm from next door. The stone cottage. I'm Ana.

Yebo, ma'am, she said, bending down slowly to pick up the duster, one hand on her back. You want *Nkosaan* Franz?

The dogs had lumbered across and were alternating between sniffing her ankles and giving half-hearted barks.

Is he here? I'd like to use the telephone. Mine's out of order.

He's not here, ma'am. But come, use the phone, it's not a problem.

The insurance broker said he'd look into it. Took down the van der Veers' telephone number and said he'd leave a message there for her to call him. She took out a coin and placed it next to the telephone, looked around for a pen and a scrap of paper so that she could leave a note for Franz. A photograph of two young men caught her eye. They were on a boat, each holding up a fish by the tail. She leaned forward instinctively, squinting to see if she could recognise Franz. Yes, there he was, more hair, a suntan, laughing. The youth at his side as tall as he, his blond hair, half wet on his shoulders, a square face.

They don't look like that anymore. The black lady was suddenly in the room.

Who is . . . is this Franz?

Ja, ma'am. Is *Nkosaan* Franz and *Nkosana* Daniel when he was small. Lake Kariba. You know it? Rhodesia. Zimbabwe.

I've heard of it. Daniel doesn't look small.

The black lady laughed, her ample breasts heaving in delighted accord. *Yebo, Nkosana* Daniel is more big than *Nkosaan* Franz. But for me – I know him since he was baby – for me he is always the young one.

They look happy.

I don't know. Many stories since that time. Now they don't look like that anymore.

FOUR

IT WAS LATE the following day that Franz found her curled up in her father's chair, her face hidden behind a book.

Knock, knock, he said, walking in. Oh, there you are. He smiled. The picture seemed to amuse him.

A man called for you this afternoon, something about an insurance policy, he said.

Oh, she replied, setting the book down and straightening up. That was quick for the third world. I wasn't expecting to hear so soon. Sorry to drag you over here.

Not at all. I told him you'd call back. If you hurry you'll still catch him before he goes home. Then stay for a drink if you like.

So, the third world, huh? he cocked his head and watched her as they waded through the grass to his house.

Third world? she said, aware that the hem of his suit pants were getting filthy from the wet grass.

You said the gentleman's response was quick for the third world. I take it you find this country a little primitive?

Oh dear, did I say that? She tilted her head, trying to remember. Did I offend you? I'm so sorry.

It's okay, he said. I'm just curious.

Actually, I don't think that. I'm just very familiar with

the expression. Especially when it comes to South Africa. She reached up to clutch her hair, a habit she'd had since a child, something for her hands to do. But it was gone. Nothing to hold on to.

I think it makes you feel better when you're far away if you can say things like that, she continued. You know, to go on about the crime, the economy. It helps you cope.

I can imagine, he offered. Especially if you can roll your eyes when you say it.

The two bulldogs lumbered across the grass.

George! Clementine! Paws! said Franz, but already it was too late, their muddy imprints all over her jeans and T-shirt.

It's fine, she said. I prefer the approval of animals and children.

The money would be released within a couple of months. There were some administrative requirements, proof of death, that she was the sole beneficiary of the estate.

You're welcome to use my fax machine, and telephone, whatever you need, he said, pouring himself a glass of red wine. You? He tilted the wine towards her.

Thank you, okay. And thanks for the offer. But I suppose I should get my father's phone line reinstated.

It's your house, your phone now. You can do whatever you like.

She took off her shoes and settled herself in to the enormous sofa, cross-legged, then took the wine goblet from him and held it by its stem, staring ahead. She hadn't thought of it quite like that. It was her house now. She had her own house. She would need to speak to Michael at some stage soon. She sighed as he sat down next to her.

To third world countries? she offered.

He lifted his glass and smiled. And those who seek asylum in them. Reminds me, he reckons he's coming in a couple of weeks.

Who?

My brother. This time from Burkina Faso.

Oh yes, the wall. Shouldn't I be contributing something towards that?

I'll send you an account, he grinned. Just then his mobile phone rang.

Excuse me, he said, taking the call. While he promised somebody on the other end to be at a meeting the following evening, she noticed a black square book beneath what looked like architecture magazines, lying on the coffee table. She took it out from under the pile and paged through the mostly black and white photos. Several taken in arid areas she did not recognise. Dusty mosques and markets, rows of huts, corrugated iron, carcasses hanging in the street. There were no captions, no text. Then suddenly a photo of a woman in an open coat, mid-stride, walking along what looked like a canal in Venice, biting into a plum. It could have been in black and white, she thought, the grey clouds, the canals. Except for the bruise of the plum, the stain on the woman's mouth. With her distracted gaze, her air of preoccupation, she looked like a woman with a secret. She closed the book to see who the photographer was, keeping the place with her index finger. The book had no title, simply the name: Daniel van der Veer.

Wretched committees, Franz sighed, hanging up. Indigenous minorities. That's his so-called speciality.

Who?

Daniel. He's a visual anthropologist. Specialises in indigenous minorities.

And these are his photographs?

Oh, you found that. Yes. He did that a long time ago. Before he started making films.

Are you pleased? she said.

Pleased?

That he's coming.

He was silent for a while. It'll be good to get the wall done, I suppose, he finally answered.

I don't think I've ever met a visual anthropologist.

Oh no, I don't think so. He gave a little laugh, took a slug of wine.

What?

Not a good idea. To meet this one. Daniel . . . doesn't like women.

She was quiet for a few moments, toying with her wine glass, swirling her thoughts.

I don't know that I do either, she said.

No, really, you must stay out of his way. He's nothing short of bloody rude to them. I'll spend my life apologising. Really, Ana, do yourself a favour.

He stood up and refilled his glass, even though he'd hardly touched it.

Does he like men? she asked.

No, no. It's not like that. He was married once, but she died a long time ago. It was pretty much since then. But even before he became a complete misogynist, he was strange. Odd. You know, every family has one.

She didn't know, she thought. What was his wife like?

Flirtatious, he said. Not his type.

Who's his type?

I don't know. Like I say, he's peculiar. Clever, mind you. Taught himself to read. Nobody's quite sure how, and today when you ask him, he doesn't answer. I suspect it was through graffiti.

33

She gave a little laugh. Were you exposed to much?

My parents travelled quite a bit. They'd leave us with Angelina. As I think I told you, she's always been like part of the family, more motherly than our own. Daniel adored her. Her brother, a tall, lean man with Siamese cat cheekbones, would arrive once a month – those months when my parents were at home – in his derelict, repainted blue Valiant to pick her up and take her home. Once, when he was around four and a half, Daniel managed to get into the car. He hid behind the seat, crouched under a pile of newspapers. They only found him when they got back to the township where they were staying at the time.

She smiled. That must have caused quite a stir.

Angelina went immediately to the trading store and called my mother. I can just imagine it. As you've seen, Angelina is not a small woman – she needs very large breasts to cover an equally large heart. Huge sense of humour, but no nonsense. Not even from Daniel. I can see her marching across some dusty road, gripping Daniel's grubby arm in her strong hand, dragging him to the phone, his little legs stiff with refusal, to explain to my mother what he'd done. Mom spoke to Daniel, who insisted that he wanted to visit Angelina's house. Strangely enough she agreed. It was very out of character. When Daniel came home with Angelina on the Sunday night, he was covered in paint and knew how to spell *free*. Later we discovered that Angelina's youngest brother, Bright, was a graffiti artist, amongst other things. Some years later he joined the ANC and got himself arrested.

So Daniel probably taught himself to read.

Yes, after that little jaunt, he read everything he could lay his hands on – signposts, scraps of newspaper, headlines, slowly sounding out the words. And then, when he was nine, he built himself a radio. You know, back in the days when we called it a wireless.

She nodded. Sounds like it worked too.

Oh, it worked all right. He found out how to do it from some moth-eaten book he'd dug out of the cellar. Followed the instructions to a T, and when he'd finished the task, he could pick up not only local stations, but shortwave too. At night, when it was still and there was less interference, I'd walk in and find him listening to stations like Radio Moscow and Radio Havana, Cuba.

That's extraordinary. I didn't realise they were in English.

Oh yes. What I didn't know then, is that he was writing off to them for free material they were offering. Or that Rhodesian-born comrade Daniel van der Veer from Cape Town had been added to their mailing lists. They had no idea that the enthusiast to whom they were sending communist manifestos and Marx's theories was only nine years old.

She laughed. But would he actually have *read* them?

Does the pope wear a funny hat?

She stared at him.

Every last word. By the time he was ten he'd announced that he was a communist.

Your parents must have had a big surprise.

They never knew. I only found out much later. I read it in a newspaper article somewhere and asked him if it were true. He never answered, of course, secretive little bastard, but I could see from his face that it was.

Would you have stopped him?

Yes, most likely. It was illegal. That was probably the only attraction for him. He could have got us all into terrible trouble. I don't like a fuss. I like order as much as Daniel loves chaos.

She noticed for the first time a scar across his left temple. It seemed incongruous with the clean lines of his face, his straight nose, evenly spaced eyes. His hair was thinning slightly on top, but even that added something – was it refinement? – to him. Or maybe it was the thin-rimmed glasses, hard to tell. She was about to leave when Angelina appeared at the door.

Nkosaan, will the little missus be staying for dinner?

No, no, she said. I must go. I've overstayed anyway. You've been very kind.

Not at all, he said. And you'd be most welcome to stay – you look like you could use some feeding – the only thing is, I've got a meeting tonight, so if you do, you'll have to excuse me if I eat and run.

Thanks, both of you, but no. Another meeting?

Ja, you tell him, said Angelina, clearing away their wine glasses. This is why you get headache. You don't want to listen.

He smiled, then turned back to her. I'm involved in the organisation of a low-cost housing scheme. I try to get volunteer architects and engineers to do their bit, but it's a bit chaotic sometimes. When people aren't being paid, they tend to take liberties. Anyway, never mind. Next time you must stay. I hope that will be soon.

FIVE

SHE WAS EIGHTEEN when she and Michael arrived in London. It was the first time she had been in an aeroplane. Late February. Her first impression was of people walking, running, rush hour, a shiver of activity, a blur of legs and feet. And coats and hats and umbrellas squashed in with gypsies jostling for money on the tube. Mind the gap. The size, the scale, of London made her panic. Museums of every variety that went on for blocks, bookshops with their different floors and countless titles and special offers, the constant movement and flow of buses, taxis, opinions. When Michael went off to work, she walked and walked but somehow never arrived, never understood the maps, the maze of this heartbeat. The shops boasted every brand name she had ever seen, and many more she hadn't. Designer labels, pick your look, be who you want to be. But who? The beach girl she'd left behind in Cape Town had no place in this grid. Her wraparound skirts, sarongs and kikois, the cowrie anklet, floaty ponchos in the winter, could survive neither the weather nor the vortex of acceptable trends. She tried not to think of home, unsure when she and Michael would have enough money to be able to return for a visit. But now and then she would overhear an Irish accent, a stranger passing, and long to follow the voice – *stop, wait* – and hide for a minute in its ebb and flow.

It was a while, and the arrival of spring, before London took her seriously enough to allow her the opportunity of looking through some of its more beautiful windows. The garden at Fenton House, where grass grew wild in the orchard and wisteria covered the benches. The view from Waterloo Bridge – but you had to walk from north to south – with Westminster Cathedral on the right, St Paul's on the left and Canary Wharf in the distance. And in late summer, swimming in the ponds at Hampstead Heath. The larger museums were generally too overwhelming, but the smaller ones she loved. Her favourite, the Sir John Soane's, a Georgian townhouse built on a square, with plaster casts, antiques and sculptures, and best of all, Hogarth's panels of *The Rake's Progress*. Then there were the street names. If you paid attention, you could always find one to match your mood. *Content Street* – somewhat short, only three or four houses long – *Change Alley, Old Paradise Street* or even *Bleeding Heart Yard*.

They moved to the flat in Barnes after their honeymoon. Although the block itself was unremarkable – a seventies special in functional face brick – it had a separate bedroom and lounge, and overlooked a park. Before then, they had shared accommodation; a room below road level, the grit and the rain ground into her by the constant footfall of pedestrians. The Barnes flat with its outlook of trees and the occasional bickering of pigeons, marked not only their new marital status, but somehow their commitment to stay and become part of the fabric and structure of the United Kingdom too.

But the walls were thin, and the plumbing cantankerous. Every time a neighbour had a shower, ran a bath, or flushed a toilet, the occasion was shared throughout the building, in growls and reverberations, sometimes at three or four in the morning.

And then there was Mr Sinclair. Hard of hearing, Basil Sinclair lived in the flat to the right. The one with the ornate bronze door knocker in the shape of a crouching lion. There would be silence from the flat for weeks at a time, and then all of a sudden he would be back, all pink and portly, and, after banging at her door, announce that he was back from the Vatican.

We must have a glass of wine, he would articulate loudly, as though sincerity were measured in decibels. I must have you over.

But the invitation never materialised, and simply became another meaningless line in the ritual of her daily conversations. *How are you? Fine, thank you.* Then he would disappear behind his door, and she would wait – sometimes half an hour, sometimes less – to hear excerpts from his great passion, the recorded speeches of Churchill, booming through the walls like an irascible ghost.

On Saturdays there were often weddings. The same score would filter up from the stone Presbyterian church almost every week. Mendelssohn's *Wedding March* thumped out as though the future of the marriage depended on it, while expensive cars would deliver made-up and hairsprayed brides. Like something out of Madame Tussauds, she thought, watching from her window, as they alighted from the vehicles.

At first, her father called her once a month. She would wait for it for days before it came. Once he'd called as the marriage ceremony was beginning. What's that? he asked. What's that awful noise?

Weekly wedding, she said. Gets a bit much. Surely you can't hear that, Sam?

Organ's out of tune, he said.

She never knew whether he'd really heard the false notes or not. But he was not a man who liked the telephone much, and for the most part the repetitiveness of the short conversations grew predictable with their stock questions and replies.

The frequency of the calls diminished. It was several months since her last, ordinary chat with him. She'd been over it again and again in her head, trying to patch the ragged snatches together, in case he'd given some clue she'd missed, some vital subtitle.

The weather was turning, he'd said. There were leaves to mulch. And a woman had been taken by a great white shark in Fishhoek while taking an early morning swim. People on the beach saw it breach right out of the water then smack down onto the poor soul. Nothing left except her red swimming cap. Of course, they wanted to put in more shark nets, a travesty, what that does to the dolphins and seals. And how was she? Did she play much these days?

She loved it that he never asked whether she'd found a job, kept the conversation uncomplicated. Age had added some hoarse and raspy strains to his voice.

Your voice needs tuning, Sam, she'd said.

Is that so, dear? She could hear the wry smile. Have a tuning fork then?

All this she played over and over again in her mind. Each phrase, every nuance, she repeated to herself whenever she could, in case she forgot something and it fell through the spaces, as though by repetition she could hold and protect their final exchange in her hands. Still, she struggled to find it – any suggestion at all amongst what he'd said that even vaguely hinted at the small fact that he was dying.

She had left for London with Michael before completing her music degree. But she hoped she could audition for an orchestra anyway. Michael did too. He painted a picture of living a bohemian lifestyle, with other artists, poets, musicians who were far from home, protesting against injustice. He imagined smoky, late-night meetings – readings, recitals, debates – with people who brought with them stories of pain and triumph. By refusing to go to the army, and thereby making a stand against the system, he felt he had given the two of them the moral right to belong in such company. It was then up to her to provide the talent, the entry ticket, into these circles of quasi-underground appeal. He had no doubt it would all unfold, that they would live their lives with passion and meaning, once she started to play.

And maybe it would have, she thought, if she had been accepted. But in spite of her disciplined daily practice the door to the London music scene seemed closed; the auditions simply a gap, a glimpse, into a world in which she was invisible. She wished she could forget her first few auditions in London. Could forget standing before a panel, fingers faltering and breath shallow, feeling like a peasant dining at the table of the Queen. Knowing how important the outcome was to Michael, to their union, to the life they had dreamt for themselves. Later knowing that this is the banquet on which our demons feed.

And then, after the failed job application in South Africa, IFDA promoted him, from programme manager to programme director, which meant a great deal more travelling, a sizeable pay increase, and a car. His job took him to many countries, sometimes for weeks at a time. Once in a while, if he were working somewhere on the continent, he would try to arrange for her to join him. But most often, if not in London, he was in Paris, where the company had an office with a small loft apartment for employees in the 13ᵗʰ arrondissement.

Paris. It wasn't the cafés and the clichés, although even those had their charm. It wasn't the Eiffel Tower or the Louvre. Or even the river. It was hard to pinpoint what it was about that city that energised her, each newly discovered street, new experience, smell of food and diesel. She must have lived there before, she decided. On each corner she imagined she could feel nuances of lives almost remembered. Or maybe she would do so in the future, and time was reversing, offering her a sample, a foretaste. At times, she thought it was the light, particularly in summer, late afternoons, falling liquid through the linden leaves. After the low clouds of London, it was almost as though the clarity made her feel taller. The ceilings in the churches and museums seemed unusually high. To let it all in – the light – she figured. So that even with the swarms of tourists clicking and aah-ing, she felt she could exhale. And smile, and drink Sancerre and wear soft blouses and silly sandals, and sometimes sing swaying songs, *The Girl from Ipanema*. Their honeymoon was spent in a small hotel, Hôtel de l'Espoir, tucked away down a side street on the Left Bank, in the *cinquième*. The bed with the *bienvenue* chocolate on their pillows. The white tiled bathroom with the French ultramarine towels. The window with its view of rooftops – a junkyard of tiles like dirty shells gleaming and reflecting, television aerials and occasional satellite dishes, their faces turned upwards as though expecting a kiss. The breakfasts *à la chambre,* the silver coffee pot and *pains au chocolat*. The lady hotel owner with the beehive hair and electric-blue eyeshadow and the grizzled husband, *bonjour madame, bonjour monsieur*, as she and Michael stepped out into the street.

Or perhaps it was because in Paris she was on holiday; free for a few days from the sense of failure that her life in London carried for her. Free from her rigorous practice routine. And in love. Paris courted her with its beauty and its confidence – its wrought-iron balconies and begonias, its old French cars stacked up one behind the other without an inch to move between, its poets and painters, nights jackknifed with passion, stories of war. So many histories rubbing shoulders on every corner. Such arrogance. Such pride. Once, while waiting for the métro, she saw a vagrant reading Voltaire.

Or maybe it was simply that in Paris, where she did not know French, she could hide. Without expectations, a fixed address, recognisable words that identified her world, there were no mirrors to reflect her. She could freefall between the lines of languages, unaccountable to any linear arrangement of thought, free to vibrate with the city's pulse and breath. The most important things are hardest to find words for, her father once said. That's why people make music.

And perhaps poetry, she thought. The rhythm and texture behind the words the real hypnosis. To her, Paris was a poem. She and Michael would spend hours walking, absorbing the tempo and cadences, the flavours and tones. Sometimes they would buy baguettes and head for the Jardin du Luxembourg, to La Fontaine Médicis, where they would sit in silence, their thoughts swirling in the sound of water, under the plane trees. She would watch the doomed marble lovers, Acis et Galatée, and shiver. The statues reflected the simple myth, its tragic triangle, with perfect grace. She'd shift closer to Michael and reach for his hand. She could feel the frailty of that moment. Feel the fragility of the sea nymphs' bliss, as they folded into one another, intertwined, while the bronze Polyphemus, dark and weathered, hovered jealously overhead, a rock in his hand, waiting to destroy them. Waiting.

Then there was the daily market in rue Mouffetard, close to the hotel. The street, a remnant of an old Roman road, was defined by small twelfth-century buildings and lined with table after table of fresh produce – chickens, meat, cheese, fruit. Merchants chatted and sold, now and then flirted with passers-by, shooing away birds from the cobbled stones. She remembered the first time she found it, she felt she had stepped back into the Middle Ages. She wandered some way up the street, trying some cheese, buying a punnet of wild cherries, turning away hurriedly and rushing to catch up with Michael, after a young fruit vendor had smiled at her, winked, then narrowed his eyes and said *ravissante*. A little further on, she found a wine shop. She lingered a while over the baskets of bottles outside, trying to understand the poems the owner wrote longhand and placed amongst them to describe each varietal. That day, she saw him at his desk, the wine-poet, scratching his head, before looking up and speaking to her in French. She thought she caught the word *vignes*.

I don't know, she apologised. English.

It's okay, he said, looking up, his face suddenly opening as she slipped back into the street.

Some way up and to the left, just before the Place Contrescarpe – the square that Hemingway immortalised, of course, said Michael – and before église Saint-Etienne-du-Mont, was a tiny walkway, rue du Pot-de-Fer.

Come, you must see it, said Michael, dragging her in.

She found the street dark and uneven, lit up here and there with lanterns and small leaded windows. Now and again, a staircase would appear like an invitation. And then a signboard *Maison des Trois Thés*.

Let's give it a try, said Michael.

The menu was extensive, the two oriental ladies who served there small and precise. It was clear from the grave expressions on their faces that tea was a serious matter. An art form. A ritual. With over seven hundred kinds from which to choose, each exquisitely blended, she took advice from Michael, who took advice from the older of the pair, and ordered a pot of the green variety. The drinking process was then explained to them in English, by the younger of the two. The doll woman's pencilled eyebrows flew up and down, her mouth a perfect Cupid's bow, stop-sign coloured, as she stressed that on no account – *no* account – should the leaves *ever* come into contact with boiling water, which burnt them and destroyed the flavour. After that, she and Michael waited a while for the tea to draw. When he thought it was ready – she waited for him to nod – she lifted the cup to her mouth a few times, not daring to drink at first, in case it was too hot, in case they had not waited long enough, in case she offended the tea police. She remembered having no idea that several cups of tea could leave her shaking as much as if she'd been mainlining espressos all day.

Their honeymoon had been short, only three days. They had visited what Michael assured her were the Louvre's three leading ladies the *Mona Lisa* – who was smaller than she expected – the *Venus de Milo* – who was larger, and the *Winged Victory of Samothrace*. He told her that when the *Paris Review* was first launched in the fifties, shortly after Bannister did the four-minute mile, the editor George Plimpton would only consider employees who could do the six-minute Louvre, which meant getting there really early, sprinting past all three works and getting back to the taxi within six minutes.

They drank coffees at sidewalk cafés, where they sat alongside one another – not opposite – and watched people, dogs, birds.

Look, Ana. *Les moineaux*. It means little monks, said Michael, pointing to the tiny brown sparrows as they dipped and picked up crumbs from the pavements. He had studied French Literature at university, and enjoyed explaining what he knew. They had attended an organ recital at Saint-Étienne-du-Mont, on the corner of rue Clovis, by the Panthéon. A church where Sainte Geneviève's tomb lay.

Sainte Geneviève was the patron saint of Paris, Michael explained. She lived in the fifth century and was controversial because of her vision and the miracles she facilitated – one of which involved saving Paris from Attila's hordes. When Paris was blockaded by Childéric, she led a convoy of boats provisioning the city. He added that there was considerable debate whether it was her prayers or the miraculous supply of wine she provided to the workmen that secured the construction of a basilica over the tomb of Saint Denis.

After the recital, they bought red prayer candles, lit them, then knelt on the red velvet, heads bowed.

What did you pray? he asked.

It's a secret, she said.

Tell me.

But it's a secret.

Come on, he insisted.

That we could both live in Paris one day. I prayed to Sainte Geneviève. It seems that would be a small thing for her.

He remained silent, then took her hand and pulled her into the vestry to kiss her.

Later that night, he took a new prayer candle from his pocket. For you, he said. From Sainte Geneviève.

When he started travelling there more frequently for work, she begged him to relocate, promised to learn French, suggested it might be easier for her to find employment there. But he said it was not sensible. IFDA's head offices were in London. As a director, he needed that to be his base. But she could visit often, he promised. He would do his best to get her over there as frequently as possible.

She thought back to the last few minutes of her visit only a few weeks ago. It was always like this, leaving. The last goodbye almost abrupt – please Ana, go quickly now – the turning away. No scenes. Then the taxi would arrive to whisk her away. Like contractions the signs to the airport would come more frequently. She'd be aware of worlds dividing and multiplying and a thousand spaces between. For a short time he would linger in her, in her movements, her clothes, her hair – she'd still smell of him. And then departure halls, planes, connections and all too quickly he would have disappeared, transmuted once again into memory. A voice on the phone in the crypt of the night.

Did I wake you?

She could remember looking out from the taxi as it sped to the airport at dusk. It was summer, still light. The highways peeled away from her on all sides, propelling her into the industrial areas. Out. Away.

Expelled into the ether. The seats in the taxi were torn. Other people's fingers tense as her own, perhaps? A last grapple to hold on, to bear down. The driver stared ahead unblinking. Life-worn.

She could still smell it, that taxi, smell the cigarette ends and stale smoke. This, in spite of the *espace sans tabac* warning and the white plastic sticker with a red cross over it. The smell of obscurity. Of transience. The driver sped and braked and indicated to change lanes through the traffic. Fast and slow past the two high mirror-glass buildings on the outskirts of the city, Les Mercuriales, in their boxy faces reflections of a city always moving. As she left the kernel of congestion behind he flicked on the radio and settled back slightly into his seat, glancing at her in the rear-view mirror. She wondered what he saw, the travelling-for-money man, as French adverts blared through on the radio. She reached into her handbag for a pen, for a poem. And on the back of an old envelope tried to find the rhythm for what she'd left behind.

SIX

A FEW DAYS after the phone was reconnected, she called him on his mobile.

Michael?

And then the tirade she knew was waiting.

Ana. My God, what on earth . . .? You leave a message on my phone to say your father's dead, that you're going back to Cape Town, and then . . . nothing, I've tried to call I don't know how many times, but I couldn't get through, typical bloody South African phones, you could've at least let me know you'd arrived safely, I've been worried sick, what's got into . . .

Sorry. I didn't mean . . .

Didn't mean *what*? Are you out of your . . .

My father died, Michael.

Yes, I know, you said so. I'm sorry about that, really, but does that mean you have to make everybody else's life a misery?

A misery? He was my father.

Yes, I know, I know. Okay, never mind. When are you coming home?

I don't know. She wanted to say she did not know where that was.

What do you mean you don't know?

I mean I don't know, she repeated.

Look, he began. You can't . . .

Where are you, London?

Yes. Doesn't matter. You can't just . . .

Yes, I know. I need to go now, Michael.

She could imagine his neat and lanky frame, suited and white-shirted, in his office. Waves of traffic swimming up from the street, the buzz of the neon light above him. His desk lit up in circles by a reading light, the computer monitor at the one corner of the desk, files in stacks on the other, Costa coffee cups, the milky dregs of cappuccino still lining the rims. How far you've drifted from the blue-eyed boy I met with his surfboard here on Noordhoek Beach, she thought. The boy with the mouth wide and free as a bird in flight. The boy who knew how to play, to dream.

Still she blamed herself. Had she found a job in London things may have been different. But after the first year of auditions, her sense of failure was bigger than her motivation. Each time, she would leave the flat intent on giving it all she had. She even took to popping beta-blockers that paralysed the symptoms of fear – hands perspiring so that her fingers kept sliding off the keys, mouth so dry and breath shallow. But as she approached the venue, something would rise up within her. She could already see the bare room, the singular music stand and the congenial but distant decision-makers, shaking their heads ever so slightly, occasionally smiling at her with a terrible kindness. She would leave the premises, scurry off to a remote café for a coffee, and with head bent staring at the design on the paper cup consider that the only thing worse than rejection was pity. Then she tried for more theatrical positions – positions where she would play for musicals, children's performances, but even these gave her stage fright, and in the end all she did was stand outside the practice rooms, listening to the other candidates warming up. And then she stopped going altogether. It was cancelled, she'd lie to Michael. But secretly, she suspected that even the buskers, their upturned hats on street corners, were better than she. After all, if she had been any good at it, she might have brought her father back to life.

She loved the flute, your mother.

Brought back to life the man whose soul had flown away with that woman when she died. That woman whose silence pervaded his every thought. Whose fatal fragility had sliced to the very quick of his breath.

She stepped out into the garden. The morning sun had been usurped by cloud, and a sharp breeze snapped at her bare arms. Still, she noticed a sudden shock of daisies, like orange stars, had sprung up at the back door. And in the distance on the grass bank by the stone wall, a choir of wild arums had started to bloom. Spring must be around the corner. From where she stood she could see the mountain, still scorched here and there, in the distance. As she wandered across a patch of lawn to some aloes, she felt her father's gratitude that the firebreak had saved the garden. When she was small, her father had taught her about indigenous plants. She'd called them *genius plants* till her memory could hold all four syllables. She remembered he'd explained that the Cape Floral Kingdom was the smallest of six in the world, with the most variety. It made her proud. It also captured her young imagination; she sensed that she lived in a unique, possibly magical Kingdom of Plants. She strongly suspected it was one which she and her father alone could access. More importantly, one in which her mother lived, he told her. He would take her by the hand and walk her through the garden, introducing her to each plant by name, as though they were people. Some delighted her again and again: Red Hot Poker, Nodding Pincushion, Blushing Bride, Elephant's Ears. After a while, she remembered the names herself, and every time she passed them she would whisper: *Protea, Erica, Aloe.* Even with him gone, she almost believed she could hear them replying.

She made her way to the wall, to an area where it was decaying. In the distance she could see Franz sitting on his stoep, the two bulldogs collapsed around his feet, their eyeballs swivelling on their paws. She waved. He beckoned to her to come across. When she reached him, reclining in his wicker chair, one of the dogs tried to bark, but after considering the strain it would take to raise her head, abandoned the effort.

Clementine, he warned.

She noticed Franz had rings under his eyes. He looked tired.

Hello, she said.

Came home early. Bloody migraine. I get them now and again.

That's awful, I'm sorry, she said. Time to slow down?

I wish I could, he smiled. Would you like some tea? He rose as she answered. Clementine staggered to her feet, bleary-eyed, and brushed her nose against his leg, ready to follow, while George rolled onto his back and stretched, four paws in the air.

Yes, she said. No, I'll get it. You sit. Please.

He sank back into his chair, his hand reaching for the back of his neck. Angelina's in the kitchen. She can help you.

The dog collapsed again.

She found Angelina rolling pastry. She was wearing the same blue African print scarf as the last time. Before she could even ask about the tea, Angelina launched in.

He doesn't learn. Every time he get sick.

Who, Franz? she said, watching as Angelina flattened the pastry with vigour.

Ja. *Nkosaan* Franz. Look now. Again the headache. Next time he's dead.

He probably needs to take a break. Does he take holidays ever?

Never. Always doing this, doing that. This committee, that one wanting, wanting. You tell him, ma'am. You help him, please ma'am. Me? I'm just old Angelina, he laugh when I tell him. You tell him, he like you, I know.

What about his brother? Isn't he coming down soon? Won't he listen to him?

Angelina rolled her eyes. Never. Those ones, they don't talk. *Nkosaan* Franz and *Nkosana* Daniel? Not for lo-o-o-ong time. *Eish*, I don't know. Daniel . . .

And suddenly she was smiling.

She returned with a fresh tea tray, in case he wanted to join her.

Angelina's worried about you, she said, settling the tray on the table and sinking into the chair. Tea?

I know, he smiled. No thanks.

Sure?

Yes. I sometimes feel a bit queasy after a migraine.

How often do you get them?

Oh, I don't know. Now and then. It's just one of those things, you know. Some people get them, some not.

Angelina thinks you're overdoing things.

She thinks she's my mother, he said with a laugh. Although she's been around longer than my mother, come to think of it.

What about her family?

Her husband used to work for us too. Wonderful in the garden, and a sort of handyman also. He died of a heart attack about fifteen years ago. It wasn't easy for them. They were ANC supporters in Natal. Zulus. There was all that faction fighting between the ANC and Inkhata at the time. The family eventually fled to Cape Town for their lives. She was the one who held it all together.

What happened to her brother?

To Bright? He didn't live with us. He was too young and volatile at that stage. My mother didn't feel safe. Then, later, he was arrested. He died in prison, nobody really knows how or why. What you hear is never the truth in those cases.

It's strange to think of her as part of such a passionate family, and yet she's your domestic.

I don't think she sees it that way. I think community was always more important to Angelina than politics or wars fought in the name of justice. Or righteousness. I think she sees us as family. I really do. She has a daughter. Clever girl. Studying law at UCT.

He stared ahead. But yes, funny things families. And what makes them. I suddenly remembered the other day, that Daniel once joined the circus.

As what?

An acrobat, apparently. One holiday – he was around eleven – he told my parents he was going to summer school, but in actual fact he had joined a visiting circus.

Her eyes widened in surprise.

They trained him, taught him all the moves. And then one weekend, my parents were walking past the large field where the circus had positioned themselves for a few months, and there was Daniel, leaping in the air.

He was already a communist. She started to smile.

Yes, a communist, then an acrobat.

You're obviously very fond of him, she said.

Daniel? No, actually. What gives you that idea?

You speak about him all the time.

He narrowed his eyes, forehead slightly furrowed.

Did you tell him? asked Angelina, when she carried the tray back to the kitchen.

To slow down? I don't think he'll listen.

The older woman shook her head.

Never listen. And never to Angelina. But someone must say. Before he die too.

Too? Who else died?

She was frying onions and small cubes of beef. The pastry lined the pie dish, waiting.

All this work, committee, helping people, she shook her head. It's not bring her back.

Who?

She's gone. *Phelile.*

Who? she asked again.

The one in the car when *Nkosaan* Franz make accident. The wife of *Nkosana* Daniel.

Family, she thought, as she walked home. Those we're born into, those we choose. *Erica, Protea, Aloe,* she whispered as she passed them. They were only days away from blooming.

Family she imagined they said in reply.

SEVEN

Since her first night back, her father's bedroom door had remained shut. His smell on his jerseys – flowers, he smelled of flowers – his pillows, the worn green blanket, these are what she could not face. By keeping the door closed, she felt that some part of him still lived. She sometimes touched the door handle, as she was passing. Not to open it, but as some kind of acknowledgement. He was still there. She had not been left behind. *Had not been left behind.*

It's a cool day. She can't be more than nine years old. She walks up a short hill after school with the other children, to wait for their parents or lift clubs, satchel on her back. The straps pull her shoulder blades down. As usual, she sits on the smoothed logs that are the fence, swinging her legs, waiting for her father. The cars come and go, scuffing up dust, doors banging, before driving off again. Within minutes, the clot of children thins out, until finally she's the last one left. She fixes her eyes on the road, wobbling a loose tooth with her tongue. He is mostly on time, her father, but occasionally she finds herself waiting, swinging her legs and wondering where he could be. She knows that sometimes if he is working on a very special instrument – a few weeks ago it happened with a viola – he could forget the time.

That's what happens if you're very lucky, he tells her.

To do something and forget the time means your soul is happy.

Her father's soul is not happy often, so when he is a little late to pick her up, she tells herself that the waiting is for a good cause.

But today's a flute day. He's never late on a flute day.

Twice a week, after school, he picks her up and takes her to Mr Trimble, where she has lessons after school. Mr Trimble is a pale, distant man who speaks in a soft voice. He does not smell of flowers. He smells of dandruff.

As she stares into the distance, her tongue still worrying her tooth, her mind starts to wander. It strikes her that something might have happened to him. If that is true, what will happen to her? She will be all alone. They will come and get her and take her away from their home. With her breath tight and high in her chest, she resolves that she will not allow that to happen. She'll run away and when they stop looking for her, give her up for dead, she'll return home, to their cottage, and live there for ever.

Still he does not come.

A lady in a shiny red car stops and leans over the passenger seat, winds down her window. Wanna lift?

But she knows that talking to strangers is wrong, and getting in their car even worse, and what if he comes one way, and she leaves another, so she says no thank you.

She wonders whether she should walk. She goes through the route in her mind. There are several uphills and what if her father comes the other way. And what about the flute she is carrying, wouldn't that get heavy? She swings her legs some more and stares at the empty road. After a while she digs in her satchel for the other half a sandwich that she didn't eat at lunchtime. It is still

lying in wax wrap. Her father always packs her lunch –
two slices of bread and cheese spread, or peanut butter,
as it is that day, and some fruit. She takes two bites, but
decides she isn't hungry after all. The food makes her
stomach hurt.

What about Mr Trimble?

She thinks about going back to the school, to phone,
but then he might arrive and think she'd left. Her
stomach ache is getting worse.

The sun shrinks behind a cloud, and the wind blows
around her like a spell. After a while two large drops of
rain break onto her flute case. She stares at them for a
few seconds, then shakes them off, jumps off the fence,
secures her satchel on her back, and starts to walk.

She is only a few steps down the road when she sees
the old Mercedes pull up. Her father jumps out and
bangs the door as if to doubly announce his presence.
He is so sorry, he says. So sorry, Ana. He has a new job
in – a special guitar, she'll love it – and he has to be extra
careful, because it's a Collings, very valuable. And if it
hadn't started to rain, he wouldn't have looked at his
watch for he doesn't know how long.

What about Mr Trimble? she says.

He bangs his forehead with his wrist and closes his
eyes. He'd clean forgotten about Mr Trimble too. They
must call him when they get home, but now she must get
in the car, it is starting to rain quite hard.

That night, to make up for it, he makes her favourite
dinner, chicken pie with sweet pumpkin and gravy. The
rain is falling steadily as they huddle by the fire with
their plates, their glasses of wine and juice. She digs into
her pie with a spoon.

Sam?

Yes, dear.

Where does God live?

God? Let me see. He lives in your heart, dear.

She chews the spoonful of pie. Mashes another piece in with the pumpkin.

Why's he so small?

Hmm, he ponders. More useful that way. Means you can take him to more places.

She stops and gulps some juice, spills a little on her chin, wipes it away with the back of her hand.

But does he grow? she asks.

Oh, I'm sure he does, dear. Everything either grows or dies.

A log collapses in the fire. He pushes his plate away for a few moments and drops another one into the flames.

Like flowers?

Like flowers.

Afterwards, he wraps her in his dark green blanket, the one he puts over his legs when it is cold and he is working, and reads her the story of the Henpecked Giant. Then he fetches the Collings guitar from the loft.

And my flute, she says. Please bring it too.

He shows her the hairline crack in the guitar, and lets her run her hands along it, and test the strings.

It's Brazilian rosewood, he tells her. Look how it shines.

How did it get a crack?

Dryness, I think.

How will you fix it?

Very carefully. With clamps and special glue.

She takes her flute from its case and holds it up against the guitar to compare its size, and shape. Then she plays him the latest piece Mr Trimble has taught her. It's quite straightforward, she hasn't even practised it much. Yet that night, tucked in between the elements, she allows her flute to transmute that simple melody into something else, something that feels peaceful. When she finally puts it down and looks over at her father, he is sleeping, the Collings guitar resting on his lap. She tastes something salty in her mouth, and feels it with her tongue. Ah ha. Her tooth has come out.

The next day she doesn't want to go to school. She wants to stay at home, with him and the guitar. She loves being near him when he is doing something that makes him happy. Loves to hear him upstairs humming, or singing. All right, he says. It can't hurt just this once.

So she stays home and reads books and makes them tea, while he works upstairs and now and then sings bits from *The Green Fields of France*.

There are two things she can never quite understand; the first, why when her father is happiest, he sings the most mournful songs. The second, why black people at the zenith of their anger *dance*.

It was this question – *why are they dancing?* – that had pulled her into trouble three years previously. She is with her father near his old Long Street office when he bumps into an old client. They talk about pianos, the scandalous Japanese mass productions. The client mentions the tone of a baby grand he'd played as a child and still owns. Rosewood and ivory.

What's that singing, Sam?

Just a moment, dear, he says, continuing the conversation, failing at first to understand the implications in the charge of voices coming down the street.

Maybe it's the circus, she says, letting go of his hand, and heading for the music. She's never actually been to a circus. But she's given it considerable thought – the acrobats, the clowns, the animals – ever since it's been a theme at school. Sam won't take her to see one because of the animals, so now it has an additional forbidden fascination.

She runs to the next street and waits till they reach her, a mass of moving, singing, swaying, stamping bodies, carrying white placards. By the time she turns to look for her father, she is engulfed by the mob, unable to see anything but legs. She tries to flee, but in her panic, loses direction, and instead of getting out of the crowd, only immerses herself deeper. Then there is a voice on a loudspeaker and everybody starts to run. She ducks into the doorframe of a shop, huddles there with some other children, like dogs in the rain, as people run and shout and men in uniforms with sticks and moustaches chase after them. There is smoke and her eyes are stinging, and tears are streaming from them, though she is not crying. And people hold their noses, and cover their faces with handkerchiefs and a small brown boy next to her lights a match.

It makes it stop burning, he says to her, an old hand.

The road is still full of smoke and dust and big tank-like vehicles going up and down when her father comes running down the street.

Sam! she shouts.

A policeman yells something, lifts his arm to threaten him, but Sam runs straight past him.

Sam! she screams again, as he picks her up in one movement, running with her under his arm, sweat pouring through his shirt, running, running till he reaches the car.

He opens the door, seats her firmly in the passenger seat and locks her in, then runs round to the driver's side and climbs in himself, locking the door and leaning forward on the steering wheel to catch his breath, his head on his arms.

Don't, he says, heaving, his face blood red. Don't ever do that again, Ana. Not ever.

I thought it was the circus, she whispers, as he turns the ignition, wiping his forehead with his upper arm. My eyes hurt.

I suppose it *is* a kind of circus, he tries to explain a little later. He is rinsing the tear gas out of her eyes with soaking cotton wool, as she hangs over the basin.

Try to keep your eyes open, dear.

Why were they dancing? she asks. And singing?

Because they're allowed to. Because you can't make laws to stop people dancing and singing.

But why were the men with sticks chasing them?

Because the men with sticks were afraid.

Of the dancing and singing? She stood up and banged her head into his chin. Sorry.

Yes, he said, pulling a towel from the rack and drying her face.

But *why*?

Maybe because you can control everything except people's hearts. Especially when they're angry.

When she'd told Michael the story many years later, he'd been over the moon.

You were how old? Six? That must have been 1976, after the Soweto riots. You were protesting. At six years old! Good on you.

She'd tried to explain to him that she was hardly protesting, she'd simply found herself caught up in it. But he'd refused to listen.

Isn't that their favourite thing, the police? he said. Give you five minutes to disperse then twenty seconds later start opening up with tear gas and rubber bullets.

I don't know, she'd said. It was the only time, and only by accident.

She never explained to him that far more terrifying than the tear gas, the police, the dogs, the screaming, was her separation from Sam – the single inhabitant in her entire world. Those occasional days when he would allow her to stay home from school and potter round the house while he worked, that was how she liked it. Just the two of them. When she was living in London, she would think about it. Would remember how she'd tried to keep him all to herself. And then she'd wonder if it weren't the same with Michael; what she most wanted was her husband, and only him. No parties, events, social gatherings. Just the two of them, the way it was when they met.

Not that Sam Delaney did not have admirers. Two, in fact. Marge West, sent from the estate agent's. And Sally, who changed her name to Shanti.

What Marge West saw in Sam Delaney, Ana still could not fathom. Yes, it was true, he was handsome and kind and soft-spoken – but Marge West was not. To Ana she seemed bossy and overbearing. And she never stopped talking or wanting Sam to sell the cottage. She would pull up at the house – always using some pretext, which Ana, even as a child, could see through – with cakes, quiches, pies.

We made these for the office, Samuel, too many you know, thought you might use them. Don't you want to put your house on the market, what on earth do you want so much ground for? At least think about sub-dividing, you could pocket some good money. They're having a fair on the common on Saturday, Samuel, the child will love it. What's your name, young lady? Goodness, your hair's a mess. Come here, let me fix it.

Fixing things was where Marge West came unstuck. She cast a cool eye over Ana's clothing, marching upstairs into her bedroom and jerking open the cupboards.

What a mess, she said.

Ana stared at her.

And half the stuff's too small for you. Come on then, get a bag, let's sort this out.

No, she said.

What? Come on. Don't be silly, young lady. I'm only trying to help. You'll feel much better when this junk is cleared out.

I like it this way, she said. It's my junk.

Don't be silly, repeated Marge West.

But Ana had already run downstairs into the garden.

I don't like Marge West, she tells her father after such a visit.

Really? he says, polishing a violin.

Yes, she insists. I hate her.

You hate her, do you? he says, rubbing the fingerboard with a cloth. That's making her very important, isn't it?

She's not important, she says. She's an ant.

I agree with you, dear. She's an ant. Do you hate ants, then?

No.

Then not much point hating Marge West, is there? Rather save it – this hatred for Marge West – for somebody worthwhile. Somebody important.

Like who?

Oh, I don't know. Some really bad bloke. Like the Grim Reaper, or something.

Who's he?

Oh, he's just a really bad guy. But you don't have to worry about him. I'll have a strong word with him if he comes this way.

Are you sure he's a boy? she asks.

The Grim Reaper? Er, no . . . not at all sure, come to think of it, he replies. Comes in many forms, old Grim. May well be a girl too.

The next time Marge West's swanky car skids to a dusty halt outside the kitchen door, Ana is there to meet her.

It's Marge-West-Knows-Best, she calls up to her father.

When he doesn't reply she shouts even louder. It's the Grim Reaper!

Then she charges up the stairs and hides under her bed.

She never knew what transpired in that visit. Only that Marge West never visited them again.

And then there was Sally-who-became-Shanti. Blonde and delicate was how Ana remembered her. At first, Shanti's outfits mesmerised her. The glittery tops, the tiny mirrors worked into her handbags, the bindies that she'd worn between her eyebrows. Shanti was a healer. She cleansed people's auras, she'd said.

What's an aura? Ana asks.

It's the colours around your body, flower, Shanti says.

Like what? she wants to know.

Like yours is . . . yours is pink and mauve with lots of orange.

Does Sam have one too?

Sam's is beautiful. But it needs healing. Cleansing. You should come for a session, Sam.

Shanti's guitar has broken. And after her father fixes it, she starts dropping by, first for tea, then sometimes she stays for supper. She never makes excuses for being there, like Marge West. She says straightaway she's come over to find out how they are doing. And she hugs Sam and then hugs her too, her long hair fragrant.

She likes it when Shanti stays. Likes the way Shanti sings while she brushes and braids her hair, tells her stories, gives her bindies of her own.

Here you go, flower, she says, pressing the bindy between Ana's soft brows. It's to remind your third eye.

To what? Ana wants to know.

What do eyes do? says Shanti.

See! she says.

Exactly.

But even though she loves Shanti's visits, loves her soothing voice, her floaty clothes, something is bothering her.

Sam? He's sitting on his bed staring out of the window.

Yes, dear.

She sits on her haunches at his feet, her elbows on her knees, hands cupping her face as she looks up at him.

What are you doing, Sam?

Not too much. Just gathering my thoughts.

How many?

How many what, dear?

Thoughts.

Let me see. Around three. Do you think that's enough?

Sam? She starts to bounce.

Yes, dear.

What if you marry Shanti?

Marry who? her father says, his glasses falling halfway down his nose.

Shanti.

I'm not going to marry Shanti, her father says quietly.

What if you marry Shanti and have a baby? She pushes it further.

I'm not going to marry Shanti and have a baby, her father says.

Noting that she is still subdued at supper time, he tells her the story of the Children of Lir. About the King's second marriage to the wicked new wife, Aoife, who had his beloved children transformed into swans.

You see, she says.

See what? he replies.

He wasn't *supposed* to get married again.

Really? But I *like* swans, he says, buttering a slice of bread and passing it to her. Then, to stop himself from smiling at her flinty glare, he jumps up and opens the fridge to take out some milk.

All these conversations were filtering back to her. The anxieties she'd had about losing him. They'd begun as far back as then.

Why did Shanti used to be called Sally? she asks one night as he's putting her to bed.

I think that was the name she was given when she was born.

Why did she change it?

I don't know, dear. I suppose she didn't want to be called Sally anymore.

I want to change my name too, she says.

But it's a beautiful name, Ana, he says. He whispers it slowly, as though savouring every syllable. *A-na Lu-i-sa*. It's your mother's name, dear. The most beautiful name in the world.

That's why I want to change it, she says. It's *her* name. Not mine.

She remembered him standing up quickly and walking out. The room was dark.

Michael called again a few days later. She knew it would be him when she heard the ring; hesitated before she answered. But he was softer this time, his fear no longer centre stage. He said he was concerned about her, that he wanted her to come home, he worried for her safety, but that he understood if she needed to be there for a while to sort out her father's affairs. He was going to Finland for a two-week congress and would be back at the end of September. He would call her.

The beach is still lovely, she said. This morning there were whales.

Ah, the beach, she could hear that smile. Give it my love.

That afternoon she took a walk to the farm village. She needed to stock up on vegetables, tea. The only hint of the previous day's rain was the shiny light, the cold. Here and there some wildflowers declared that the season was definitely turning, and green fists of leaves were getting ready to shake on it. Through the chatter of birds, the wind, she could hear the crack of waves on the shore.

At the farmstall she found a basket and filled it with milk, tea, Cape seed loaf, cheese and vegetables. She liked shopping here, this big barn, the heavy wood, the tables and chairs where people drank coffee and read the paper. It struck her that she had not seen a news-paper since she arrived. Suddenly the idea of curling up with something to read on one of the couches in the store's loft seemed very luxurious.

She was halfway down her espresso, reading about the murder of a young woman in the City Bowl a few days before. There was a photo of her; she was small and blonde and smiling, wearing a peak cap. She looked like somebody she might know. Somebody's girlfriend. Somebody's daughter. The intruder had stabbed her then set her alight, before fleeing. Most of the house burnt down too. Nobody knew what was stolen and what went up in flames. She was trying to grasp it – it was exactly this, this daily violence that Michael wanted to leave behind – when she heard the heavy footfall of someone ascending the stairs. She looked up to see a large man, his grey hair tucked back with something that looked like it had once been a bandanna, heading for a seat in the corner. He was wearing old jeans, a stone-coloured print shirt, was sweating. With his sleeve he mopped his brow, then unstrapped the black baby he was carrying on his back and laid it on the chair. From a bag he took a fresh nappy. Within seconds he had whisked away the soiled one, rolled it up, returned the infant to its bite-size pants, hoisted it up onto his back, tied a knot at the front, and walked out.

Still holding the newspaper half on her lap half on the table, she did not move throughout the entire operation, and continued to watch as he made his way down the stairs and out of the store. The baby had not once uttered a sound. Even when someone stopped him at the door, and put a hand on his shoulder and said My God, the baby was quiet. She couldn't quite hear what the surprised man said, only caught the last part: *Nou goed dan* Daniel. Welcome home.

She drained the espresso, then stood in a line with her basket to have the fresh produce weighed.

Didn't think I'd ever see *him* here again, said a woman in front of her to another.

Hmmm, agreed the second woman. And with a baby. Think it's his?

Nah, the first woman shook her head. Too black.

Wonder if he still refuses to speak to Franz.

Can't blame him, says the first woman.

It was a long time ago. Maybe Daniel's made peace with it now.

Doubt it, says the first woman. His own brother makes a move on his wife, takes her away, then kills her off? I wouldn't.

It was an accident, Denise. Don't be so dramatic. An animal ran out in front of the car. Hardly Franz's fault.

Why are you defending him? the first woman asked, taking out a note to pay for her bread and milk.

I'm not defending him. I just don't think it's that black and white.

Never liked her anyway, Daniel's wife, said the first woman, turning to leave. Bit uppity if you ask me.

Ana hoisted the basket onto the counter.

So that explained it.

Flirtatious, Franz had said. Daniel's wife was *flirtatious*.

EIGHT

SHE WOKE AT sunrise to the sound of voices, then something like falling rocks. Still blurry from sleep, she thought of the girl she had read about in the paper, saw in her dreaming eye the smiling blonde, the blood and flames. She sat up and strained to see out of the window, squinting into the light. The noise was coming from the other side. She would either have to look from her father's bedroom window, or go outside herself.

She pulled on her jeans, now baggy round the knees and buttocks, and a sweatshirt. Rubbing her eyes, she unlocked the front door and stepped out into the cold grass. An empty wheelbarrow was lying on its side alongside a mound of rocks, on the van der Veers' side of the boundary. From somewhere further up, she could hear a repetitive *clink*. Several paces away, two men were chipping away at the stone wall with a pick and hammer. She held her hand up to her face to shield her eyes from the sun, squinting and adjusting her vision to the brightness of the morning. Through her fingers she recognised him as the man from the farmstall the day before, the one with the baby. So this must be Franz's brother. This was Daniel van der Veer. The other, a black man dressed in blue overalls, she did not know.

He glanced across at her. She started to lift her hand in a polite wave, but already he'd returned to his work, bashing even harder into the old cement, rocks falling in small avalanches all about him.

Her feet were numb from cold, so she returned to the kitchen and switched on the kettle. She made mugs of tea for the two men, pulled on her gumboots and walked over to where they were working.

Hello, she said. I'm Ana.

Daniel turned and looked at her for a moment – was it a moment? hard to tell – then carried on with his banging, leaving her, arm outstretched, holding the hot drinks.

I made some tea, she said. But he did not respond. She stopped. Waited a split second. Then she tipped the tea out and hurried back into the house.

She stayed indoors all day. She listened to the banging, and later, voices, it sounded like more men, the sound of cars. Late in the afternoon, there was a knock at the kitchen door. When she opened it, she found Daniel and the labourer.

Afternoon. I need a plug point, he said. His voice, low and very English, did not quite match the weathered skin, wiry hair.

We have a small cement mixer. We need to plug it in.

Fine, she said. Do you want to use the one in the kitchen? Over there. She pointed.

Do you have something closer? he asked. What about the garage?

I haven't been in there. There may be a plug point in there, I can't remember.

She lifted a key off a hook at the back of the kitchen door. He followed her into the garden, to the rotting wooden door of the garage, and waited as she knelt down to tackle the lock. The rust stained her hand as she tried to force the key inside. After some wrestling something clicked and it opened stiffly, some liquid running from the grooves onto her clothes.

There, she said, looking up. He was standing a little way away, staring back at the stone wall, at the day's progress. The labourer was leaning against a wooden stake, watching her from sunken eyes. She moved across, bent down and tugged the grimy door handle. The wood had expanded, the door stuck. She yanked it as hard as she could, feeling her back wrench. A tiny rusted nail flew off from somewhere and clods of dust came tumbling down.

Damn, she muttered, her right hand moving across her lower back, where she had pulled it. She tried again, but it wouldn't budge.

Do you think you could give it a try? she asked the two of them. Neither one seemed to hear.

She gave it one last heave, using both hands this time. Still it wouldn't move.

Sorry, she said again, standing aside. Not strong enough.

Hey? said Daniel. Then he walked across to the door handle, gave it two or three sharp tugs, before it creaked and lifted enough for him to get his foot beneath it, regain his balance and lift it up.

The old red Mercedes was still there. A relic from the days when cars and women were rounder, she thought. It was covered in dust, with one tyre flat. Next to it – like an eccentric relative – the motorbike with the side-car.

She stood aside watching, with the labourer, as Daniel moved along the walls, pushing away the cob-webs and the spiders, till he found the black square box and switch on the wall. He jammed the plug into the socket and switched it on, jumping as it sparked. He brushed past her, retrieving a toolbox from the long grass near the wall, and returned. Used a screwdriver to loosen the casing, and with the screws in his mouth did something with the wires, before replacing it all.

The motorbike still had a set of keys in the ignition. She leaned over it and turned them, to pass the time while he fiddled with the electricity, but there was no response. Her hand left an imprint in the dust on the leather seat.

With a slap he placed the plug back in the socket and switched it on. No spark. That's better, he said. Come on, he beckoned to the labourer, jerking his head towards the wall. Back to work.

He left the garage door open, the cable running out of it.

She returned to the house, to the sound of the cement mixer and occasional voices. They worked until sunset, and then there was silence. When she looked outside again, the stars were out and the garage door was closed.

A few hours later, another knock.

Who is it? she said.

It's me. It's Franz. Hello. Already he was trying the door handle.

She opened the door. He stood in the dark with a basket, much like the first night he had come across to introduce himself.

I have some leftovers. I raided the fridge, he said, sinking into a chair at the kitchen table.

It's your fridge. That's hardly a raid, she pointed out.

I know. It's just that, I don't know . . . I had to get out of the house.

Daniel?

He sighed. I told you. Sorry, I should have warned you again. I didn't know he was going to start on the wall so soon. He's only just arrived, I thought he'd wait a day or two and I'd have time to tell you.

What did he do with the baby? she asked.

How do you know about that?

I saw him yesterday at the farmstall.

God knows where it comes from, or why he's got it. He handed it over to Angelina. Came back and checked on it at lunchtime, according to her, but she's got it all sorted. Those two have always been incredibly close.

Whose baby is it?

Like I said, I don't know, Ana. I really don't.

What's its name? Did he tell you? Is it a boy or girl?

No. He didn't actually, he shrugged. He didn't say anything at all. I think it's a girl. Not sure.

But it's your house. You have some right to know, surely?

It's his house too. Besides, he doesn't sleep in the big house when he's here. He sleeps in one of the outside rooms. Next to Angelina's.

He gave an apologetic laugh, to pre-empt the question. I don't know why.

He took out a casserole from the basket, condensation in the lid.

Angelina made this a few days ago. It should still be fine. Do you eat lamb?

You didn't have to bring food, Franz. I could have made something.

I didn't bring food. I brought leftovers. Oh, and a bottle of red. And some chocolate.

I love red wine and chocolate, she said.

Together? He looked surprised as she nodded.

Particularly if it's mint chocolate.

Perhaps I'll try it, he said. After supper.

She went to the fridge and took out some butter, cheese, beetroot. Arranged it on the table with bread, a board and a knife.

Okay, pot luck. We can share.

She handed him the bottle opener – an old silver corkscrew stiff and tarnished. Took out some old wine glasses, the imprint of grapes frosted onto them, from the top cupboard and rinsed them, then sat down opposite him at the wooden table.

You look tired, she said.

Why, thank you, he smiled.

Well, you do. How are the headaches?

Only one this week. It arrived yesterday.

With a baby?

Exactly. He cut a slice of bread and smeared it with butter.

And how are *you*? he suddenly asked.

Fine, she answered.

Are you sure about that?

Quite sure. Thank you.

Coping with the old man . . . well, you know . . . not being here?

She sighed and forced a smile. Reached for the bottle and splashed wine into her glass.

Later that night, after Franz had left and she had washed the dishes, Michael called. He was still in Finland.

How is the congress? she asked.

It's interesting. Some good people, he replied. She could hear the fatigue in his voice too. But how are you? he said. When are you coming home, Ana?

I need to be here for a while, Michael.

Why?

I don't know properly. Not yet. I know that must be hard to understand, but do you think you could, maybe, just try?

How can I understand if you can't? he sighed. You never were much hampered by logic, were you?

It's not about logic.

No, of course not. Then what?

I don't know. I'm sorry.

I miss you, he said.

Miss what, exactly? You're never there, she said. What difference could it make?

Is that it? You're trying to punish me? he replied.

No.

You're always within an hour or so, he said. Now it feels like you're on the other side of the moon.

You're never there, Michael, she said again, slightly more emphatic this time. Maybe I feel like an hour from you, but it's different for me. I have to wait till I'm called for. Till you have space.

We've had this conversation, Ana.

I know, and you're tired, she sighed. But it's true. You're always going . . . you're always going somewhere.

I may go. It is my job, after all. But I never leave. I'm not sure I can say the same for you.

A pause.

Anyway, I don't want to have this conversation now, he added. I miss you. That's all.

NINE

THE BABY'S NAME is Tapiwa, said Franz. It's a girl.

He had arrived once again, a few days later, at supper time, a basket of food, bits and pieces he had bought at Woolworths on his way home from work. Potato salad. Chicken wings. Sushi.

So he told you then, she said, picking up some knives and forks from the rack with a dish towel and drying them off.

No, of course not. I asked Angelina.

And what's he doing with her here?

He hasn't said apparently. Just asked Angelina to help him with it.

It's a lovely name.

Apparently it's Shona. Means *we are given*.

She dealt out the knives and forks and returned to the rack for the plates.

They worked on the wall again today, he and the man helping him, she said over her shoulder.

Did he bother you?

No, no. Not at all.

Did you speak to him?

Not today. He sent the labourer over to pick up the key for the garage. They need the plug point.

I'm sorry. It's shocking. He's got no manners, said Franz.

It's fine. In fact, when the labourer dropped the key off again, he said that Daniel asked if he could fix the motorbike and side-car.

Bloody cheek! You mean he didn't come and ask you himself?

That's okay. I just think it's odd that he wants to fix it at all. It's an old wreck. I'm sure it's finished.

He shrugged. Look, I told you, I've never known what makes that guy tick. He uncorked a bottle of wine. You can tell him to f– to get lost, you know. You don't have to put up with it.

He hasn't done anything wrong, she said. I told the labourer to tell him he was welcome to give it a try. What difference does it make?

I don't know where he hooked that guy up from anyway, the labourer. Looks a bit dodgy to me.

He has blue eyes, did you notice that? Unusual for a black man.

And a big gash down his cheek. Doesn't look very savoury to me.

It's easy to get paranoid, she said. I'm sure he's all right.

The next day she went upstairs to her father's workshop. It was much the same as she remembered it. Planks of wood, all types, arranged in stacks. Sawdust shavings. Jars of coagulated varnish on a shelf in the corner, resins, tubs of beeswax and shellac. A few violas hung from a wire stretched across the room, needing to be restrung. On one wall a couple of bow saws and an antique clock. Beneath that, on a trestle table, his collection of woodwinds. She remembered them; the oboe da caccia with its bell shape, the baroque oboe from Germany made from plum wood with ivory trim, the baroque bassoon made from boxwood. She lifted her favourite, the oboe d'amore and blew into the narrow windway, remembering the husky, warm sound. A favourite of Bach, her father had said. In the corner the treadle lathe that he had hooked up to the Singer sewing machine pedal, another stand against the use of electricity. The old wooden moulding planes were stacked in shelves, on each one the name of the craftsman who had owned it.

She smiled as she read the name FINBAR O'NEILL. They had named her goldfish after him. She remembered it clearly – his bowl was in the living room next to the gramophone. It was her job to sprinkle the fish food over his bowl every day, and to say goodnight to him before she went to bed. It was also her job to read her homework to him. Her father had been quite clear about that. That Finbar O'Neill was very interested in her reading, especially the stories about Carol and Roy and the little red lorry. He particularly enjoyed repetition, he had said.

She spends hours reading – all that her seven-year-old homework can provide – over and over again.

The little red lorry went up and down the hill. Up and down the hill with pots and pans.

She also plays the flute for him, every new song that she learns from Mr Trimble, over and again.

I think he likes it, don't you? she tells her father.

He agrees, says for sure, he can tell by the jaunty way he moves his tail.

Then one day, she arrives home from school to find Finbar O'Neill floating unceremoniously on the top of the water. She goes to pieces.

Why does everybody die? she wails. Her father shakes his head and after a while says there's really only one thing for it. Verdi's Requiem. And he makes her go and put on her new shoes – the white ones that are still a bit tight around her heels – while he finds an old corduroy jacket in his cupboard, and they sit on the sofa drinking tea and paying respects.

After the requiem, they find a box – the shoebox for the white shoes – which she insists on decorating, while he digs a shallow grave in the garden. Then they put Finbar O'Neill to rest, throw dirt on his cardboard coffin, and plant bizzy Lizzies on top.

The earth laughs in flowers, Ana, he says. Don't forget. Emerson.

Finbar O'Neill had a good send-off, all those years ago, didn't he, Sam? She sighed and instinctively looked up. And with whom must I drink tea and pay respects now?

She was still in his workshop, picking up and examining each item on his workbench, imagining the last time he may have used them – the spring pliers, the bows waiting to be rehaired – when she heard the sound of a small engine, and a dog barking. It was not the occasional drilling she had grown accustomed to from the wall construction. More like a motorbike. She crossed the floor, stepping over pieces of yellowwood and some burning irons to the window, caked so thick with dust that it looked like frosting. She loosened the latch and pushed to open it. At first it stuck, swollen from the rain, then it released and sprang open. Dust and sunlight through the gap. She couldn't see much, the window would not open very far, but there was enough space to get her hand around the pane, and clean it. She went back downstairs, and found a half-used bottle of Sunlight dishwashing liquid, poured it with some Jik into a bucket with warm water, then balancing the handle as high up towards her shoulder as she could manage, she climbed back up, and with a sponge started to wash down the window. The engine stopped. Still she cleaned, coaxing the grime into the bucket, the water inside now green-brown. The light caught something in the detergent and threw colours across the room, before she took an old cloth from her father's workbench and mopped the water away. As she tossed the rag to one side, the engine started again, and through the window she saw into the van der Veers' garden. It was Daniel, driving the motorbike very slowly, with the side-car attached. In the side-seat, he had either George or Clementine, ears streaming, while the other dog chased after them. Tapiwa was strapped to him, blanketed to his chest, and every time he allowed the revs to subside, she could hear her squealing with delight. He would drive a little way, then stop, while the other dog jumped up and barked. After a while, the dog that was outside could not contain itself any longer and jumped inside too. Round and round they went, engine revving, dog barking, baby shouting with joy.

But there was another sound, one she hardly recognised, coming from inside her father's workshop, yes, from inside her. She too was laughing, peels of wild laughter filling the house, tears running down her cheeks. As though in that brief window, mad and free, some primal joy flew in.

TEN

IT HAPPENED AGAIN the following afternoon, and then two days later once more. Soon it had become a daily ritual. He packed up his tools and headed back to the big house at around four. A little later, at the first rev of the engine, she would rush up to the loft, hiking up her kikoi to climb the stairs two at a time and prop herself up with her elbows on the weighty Oregon pine window frame to watch. The motorbike and side-car, the dogs, the baby – carefully round the lawn he drove them, in a vortex of delight. Once he stopped briefly and looked up towards the cottage, as though sensing her gaze. She shrank back, fire in her cheeks.

On one of these afternoons, she needed to go to the farmstall. Decided she would wait for the engine to stop, for him to drive the vehicle back up his driveway once the antics were over. She did not have long before the farmstall would close, but the fridge was empty and she wasn't sure whether Franz would be there later or not. His impromptu supper time visits were now quite frequent. Usually they threw together whatever was in the fridge, whatever they could find, and lately he had even taken to cooking there. He found the old coal stove charming he said, smiled when he lifted the heavy cast-iron pans from their hooks on the wooden overhang. The menu varied every time. Sometimes pan-fried sole,

or gem squash stuffed with peas or sweetcorn, sometimes lamb chops and potato wedges. Fresh rosemary
from the garden. Sometimes Woolworths lasagne and
salad. Baked potatoes. Tinned guavas or peaches and
cream. He brought wine from his cellar, often with the
excuse that she was doing him an enormous favour by
drinking it.

We have to drink this one now, it's unlikely to last
another year, he would offer apologetically, handing
her a dusty bottle.

She would decant it into an old jug.

Yes, good idea. After being trapped inside that bottle
all those years, it needs to breathe, he'd say.

He never stayed long. Several nights in the week he
had meetings. Countless organisations that he belonged
to, it seemed to her. Building projects, charities.

Why do you work so hard?

Because there's so much to be done, he answered.
Einstein once said that the world is a dangerous place
not because of those who do evil, but because of those
who look on and do nothing.

Now there's a guilt trip looking for a taker, she
smiled.

No, really, he said earnestly, I often wonder, at this
famous Truth and Reconciliation Commission of ours,
all these people who stood up and confessed to
committing gross acts of cruelty, did anybody stand up
and confess to the sin of omission? Did anybody say
Forgive me everybody, I did nothing?

She lingered at the farmstall even though she had
bought her provisions, even though it was late. She read
the notice board and finally settled down at a table and
ordered an espresso. It reminded her of Paris. The rich
coffee beans, bitter. And Michael. It was already

mid-October. In Europe, the swarm of tourists would have left, the weather would be turning. She sighed. It was hard to name how she felt. To know whether it was longing, or resignation, that filled and emptied time and again.

She sometimes wondered what might have happened, how things between them might have been, had his job application in South Africa been successful years ago.

Would they even have returned to Noordhoek? She remembers how taken aback, how hurt Michael had been when he received the rejection note.

But affirmative action is just inverse racism, he'd said. That's not progress. Not equal opportunity. Show me what's in place for the poor, across every sector. Otherwise it's just the same story, different colour.

There'll be other jobs there, she'd said. You just need to try again.

Not a chance, he'd said. I can't return to that mentality. There's no room for us there anymore, can't you see? Besides, he continued later, the whole African continent has this huge inferiority complex. You know as well as I do that if anything comes from a first world country, says *imported*, it's automatically considered *better*. So how do you think it's going to boost morale if they give a whole lot of jobs to people who know very well they're not qualified to do them?

She was about to leave the farmstall, when she heard a woman call her name.

Ana. Is that you?

When she turned she recognised the long blonde hair immediately.

Shanti, she said.

Oh my, said Shanti, holding open her arms.

Shanti had hardly changed. A bit heavier around the

thighs maybe. Her skin a little looser around her jaw. And several long strands of grey around the temple. But she still had the same shiny eyes, generous smile. The same smell of incense in her hair when they hugged.

How are you, flower? said Shanti. Oh my, you're all grown up now. Still a beautiful child. I heard about Sam . . .

Yes, she said, blinking quickly, surprised at the sudden surge of emotion.

It must be so hard for you. Are you back for good?

I don't know, right now, she said.

That's fine, flower. You'll know when you need to. You can't rush these things. Can't force answers. Allow yourself to live the questions.

No, I know. It's . . . it's all a bit confusing right now, she said, smiling.

Poor baby, said Shanti, hugging her again. I have someone in the truck, so I can't stay. But come over for supper sometime, okay? Or for a treatment.

After she paid for the espresso and lifted the brown bag onto her hip like a baby, she started to walk back. She was thinking about Shanti, how good it was to see her again. Remembered her in the cottage, wafting around the kitchen, lighting incense and candles, wearing flared pants and silly sandals. At five or six – she couldn't remember exactly how old she'd been when Shanti breezed in – it was like having a fairy in the house. So much a fairy, that her father never even seemed to see her. As though she were only visible to children.

The edges of rainclouds were falling down the mountain forming mist. Cars with headlamps on. In the distance the sound of a foghorn. She started up the road towards the mountain before cutting away through the field, a shortcut to the long driveway. Poor Shanti, she thought. It must have been impossible to be in love with Sam Delaney. She could understand why she'd slowly stopped coming to the cottage. Because even though he was always around, adept at conversation, even a good friend – when it came to his heart, Sam Delaney's was six feet under.

She reached the rusted gate and put the bag on the grass so that she could open it. Leaned over to pinch out a small stone that had crept into her shoe. As she stood up again she heard the scuffle of movement in the nearby grass, and suddenly two men appeared from behind the bank. She recognised the one as the labourer who was helping Daniel with the wall, his sunken blue eyes, the gash down his cheek. Was about to greet him, when he grabbed her shoulder and hit her on the top right of her forehead.

Sound of eggs breaking, no pain as she went down with the first blow. Second guy kicking her ribs in.

They want to kill me, she remembered thinking. If they keep hitting me, kicking me, they will kill me. *It's my turn*. All those stories in the paper. All those stories that don't even make the paper. That's all this is, another one. My turn. Why isn't it sore? They will kill me, or at least rape me. It's my turn. *My number's up*.

She could hear shouting, but it was as distant as the pain. She did not know it was her own till the beating stopped. She never knew why, maybe a car came by, maybe her shouting scared them. All she knew was that they grabbed her parcel and her purse and ran away.

A blur. She knew she ended up lying on a bed at the van der Veers', Angelina appearing, disappearing, cleaning the cuts. Remembered asking to use the phone, wanting to speak to Michael, but the numbers, especially the number eight, kept enlarging and swimming in front of her. She remembered saying she needed to speak to her husband, the look of surprise on Franz's face, and policemen, and the phone ringing all the time, and Michael's phone being off, a message to say he was en route to somewhere, she thought he said Prague.

The next day things were clearer. And painful. Franz took her to his doctor, who asked too many questions, a morbid fascination for the story, when all she wanted was to sleep. Anything to stop the throbbing.

Her eyes were puffy and almost closed. The bridge of her nose swollen. A multi-coloured egg on her forehead. Look, the rainbow nation, she said.

Just an everyday mugging, people said. You're very lucky, you know. It could have been much worse. It could have been really bad. A woman is raped every eighty-five seconds in South Africa. Think what you've been spared. These days they don't think twice about killing you. Specially seeing as you knew the guy. You could recognise him in a line-up. It was in his interests to kill you. You really are very lucky.

Lucky? hissed Michael when he finally called and she told him what they said. *Lucky?* What kind of country is that, what kind of warped thinking, lily-livered people . . . your face bloated and bloodstained, a cracked sternum and three broken ribs, and that's what they call *lucky?*

Daniel never said a word to her about it. Didn't even greet her, or acknowledge her distorted face. But she later heard from Angelina that he'd gone into the squatter camp on the other side of the valley, tracked down the labourer, and had him arrested. When she went to the police station several days later, to offer to identify him, they told her that he'd escaped.

It happens, lady, said the sergeant. Sorry.

Doesn't matter anyway, said Michael when she told him. They walk free after five minutes anyway. Jails are too full.

Michael was furious. He seemed to take it personally. Ordered her to return to London. Exploded when she asked what for. Suggested that her life might be a consideration.

What life, she thought.

In the week that followed, Franz made it his business to check on her every day. Either he or Angelina would come by, usually with food. On one such occasion he asked her about Michael.

So where *is* your husband, actually? He was looking for something he could use to boil some mixed vegetables, searching the cupboards near the stove.

You know, I'm not sure. He could be in Paris, or London, depending on commitments. Here. She handed him a stainless steel pot that she'd retrieved from the drying rack.

Flashy job, he said, standing at the sink, filling it with water.

He loves it, she replied. It's wonderful when people love what they do.

But what about *you*? he queried, looking over his shoulder. Does he love you?

That's not for me to say, she said, rummaging around for some place-mats.

Odd behaviour, to allow your wife to disappear, he said.

I didn't disappear. My father died. I needed to come back, sort things out. He hasn't been happy about it at all.

Still. He's a fool to let you go. If you were my wife . . .

But I'm not, she said, a slight warning in her tone. Not your wife.

He placed the pot of water on the stove, lit the gas, then turned around and stared at her.

You could be, if you wanted. It would be very . . . nice.

I have a husband, she said, looking away. She opened the fridge and took a bottle of tomato sauce from inside the door, and placed it on the table.

They ate in silence.

After she rinsed the dishes, she asked him what was going to happen with the wall.

What do you mean? he said.

Daniel doesn't have help anymore, she said. It's a big project. He gets the rocks from the river himself. And then there are those areas, up there by the mountain, that require extra support, retaining walls. There's still quite a way to go till it's finished.

That's okay. He's a grown man. He'll survive.

I want the job, she said.

What job?

I want to assist him. With the wall next week.

What on earth for? Besides, your ribs are injured, it's a ridiculous idea, Ana.

She began drying dishes.

I can still walk, fetch things, be useful, she said.

I'd rather find you something to do at the office if you're bored, he said.

No, she said. I want to be here. To use my hands.

He looked nonplussed.

Don't forget, she added. It's my wall too.

ELEVEN

SHE LEFT THE curtains open so that she would wake with the sun.

Daniel came down from the big house, supporting a bag of Portland cement on his head with his one hand, the other holding a large, flat piece of tin. She was already waiting, dressed in an old T-shirt and a pair of crumpled shorts she had dug out from the back of her cupboard, last worn in high school, slightly mildewy.

What? he said.

I'm going to help, she answered.

He stared at her. Hair wet. Just showered, she thought.

I can't lift things while my ribs heal, she said. But I can fetch and mix.

He sighed and shrugged, dropping first the tin, then the bag of cement on the ground.

Suit yourself.

He then continued to ignore her. Cut open the bag with a Swiss army knife that he took from his pocket, threw the powder onto a large piece of tin and walked over to the garden tap.

What happened to the mixer? she asked.

Gone, he said. Stolen.

She watched as he filled an old plastic milk carton with water, and spaded some sand in with the cement, making a sizeable hollow in the middle. He poured the water into the central trough, then picked up a stick and slowly blended the mixture together. It was a bit like making dough, she thought. She knew he was satisfied with the consistency when he let the stick fall to one side, and took two rubber gloves from his pockets.

I could do that, she reckoned. I could mix mortar. But she did not ask. Instead she watched as he selected the rocks and stones, turning them to find the flat surfaces, stacking them up with the mortar, uneven sides inwards. Now and again he would go back to the tin, and turn the mixture.

I could do that too, she thought.

During the course of the morning, he remixed the powder, sand and water several times. At lunchtime, when he had used every last scraping of the last batch, he disappeared without explanation into the big house, returning half an hour later to continue.

She sat on a rock as he worked, watching as he laid each stone, one above the other. Twice he disappeared with the rusty wheelbarrow, returning with it stacked high with rocks. She was sure he was getting them from the river – they were often very smooth, their edges water-rounded. But again she did not ask; he had made it clear that he did not want conversation. Her mind flashed back to the London coffee shops where she would seek refuge after an audition. Was this rejection? She supposed so. But a different variety – rejection in its purest form. Uncontaminated by pity. Uncontaminated by anything to do with her at all. Which is why, she figured, she could almost stand it.

The next morning was exactly the same. Except this time he didn't say anything at all. She did not budge. Sat on the rock in her shorts and a T-shirt, a bandanna, and later her father's straw hat, on her head. Even during lunchtime, when he wiped the sweat from his forehead with his arm and disappeared into the big house, she waited. Took out some sandwiches she had made, squeezed her eyes open and shut to see if the numbness was starting to ease. After half an hour or so, she watched him returning, walking towards her in the heat of the day. In the distance she could make out that he was carrying a bundle, something like a small sack. As he drew nearer she saw it was Tapiwa.

Here, he said, handing her the baby and a little bag. Angelina's busy this afternoon. If you want to help, look after Tapiwa.

She took Tapiwa, her fat little legs bicycling in the air, onto her lap. The baby did not cry, stared at her and dribbled, tufts of hair in little clumps.

She'll need a hat, she said.

In the bag, the reply.

She set the baby on the grass, took out a tiny square blanket, a pink hat, a bottle and some nappies.

We should find a tree, Tapiwa, it's getting hot. Look there's one. Over there, she said, pointing.

As she lifted the baby and headed for the shade, Tapiwa started to protest. Moved over onto her knees to push herself up.

Come on, Tapiwa, she said. It'll be hot in the sun.

But Tapiwa was twisting her floppy doll body around, her arms jutting out at right angles towards Daniel.

Da-Da-Da-neee, she said in a small, husky voice.

He dropped the rock. Gloves caked with mortar, dry and wet, he walked towards her, lowering his face to hers.

Danny's here, he said in a low voice, kissing her shiny cheek.

Then he pulled a glove off, and held out a calloused and freckled hand. She grasped his little finger as he stood to his full height.

Stay a bit closer if you can, he said. Make a plan.

She rocked the baby on her hip, thinking. It was early November, still cool enough not to worry too much about the sun. But it might get uncomfortable as the afternoon progressed. After a while she propped her up against the bag, facing Daniel, and looked around for a sturdy stick, eventually finding a thin branch.

May I borrow a hammer? she asked.

Toolbox, he replied without turning to face her.

With one eye on Tapiwa – who gazed unrelentingly at Daniel as she rocked and bounced on her nappy, blowing and humming, her hand outstretched, opening and closing like a heartbeat – she banged the stick into the earth, then attached one end of the blanket to the stick, the other spread over a bush.

Dan-dan-dan, said Tapiwa. Dan-dan-dan-nee-ee.

TWELVE

HE DIDN'T BRING Tapiwa the following day.

Angelina, he replied, bending down to knife open a bag of cement, when she asked where the child was. She decided to ask Angelina if she needed help. She found her in the kitchen, Tapiwa sitting on her nappy, rocking to and fro, while Angelina chopped onions and sang, *Tula baba, tula sana.*

It's like having my daughter back again – small, not so cheeky.

What's your daughter's name?

Kwezi, she said, handing Ana a knife and an onion. It means *bright morning star.*

She chopped for a while, then, taking a break while she waited for her eyes to stop stinging, she asked, Don't you ever miss your family, Angelina?

Me? said Angelina. Ja. But I see my daughter. Kwezi is a strong girl. The men in my family. *Eish*, nothing but trouble. She laughed and shook her head, wiping her onion eyes with her sleeve.

I love the way you laugh, said Ana. With your whole body.

Ja, said Angelina, starting to peel some carrots. When white people laugh it is from their teeth, like hyena. When black people laugh it's from their stomach, she said, patting her belly. Even maybe from the soles of their feet. That's when you know the ancestors are laughing too.

If I said that . . . said Ana.

You'd be racist, admonished Angelina.

Tapiwa started to chortle.

Ja, the older woman continued. My daughter. My daughter Kwezi is at UCT. Clever. Kwezi say she don't want black South African man for boyfriend. *Aikhona*. She like those ones from Zimbabwe, from Ghana, Congo, places like these. Or even white one. She say black South African man make problem.

Why?

She say they still want to be number one. She say at university, black women, they smart. They sick of always must know their place. All those years with other government, now they must have same story with men? *Aikhona*. But wait, she said, scraping the chopped onion into a large cast-iron pot where it sizzled and spat, banging the fork against the rim. These new black women in this country. Strong. Beautiful. Wait and see. They will make it change, this place.

The following day, she reverted to sitting on her rock watching him work. He was meticulous in his routine of sorting the rocks, mixing the mortar, laying each one as carefully as possible, and in places where there were banks, and the wall needed something extra, using wire mesh as support, till the mortar dried. Occasionally he would place a hand on his lower back and stretch as far as he could to one side. In the heat of the day he would have his shirt hanging down at the back, still tucked into his jeans, or throw it onto the grass. Other times, if he didn't have a bandanna, he took it and wrapped it around his head in a turban. His skin was weather-beaten, sun spots on his back.

She grew tired of waiting. Took a piece of wire and started doodling, making shapes; a cow, an elephant, a stick man. Then suddenly it occurred to her; she had all the materials necessary to make a statue – something for the garden. She could shape the core out of wire, then clad it with mortar. She could make something in the style of the Owl House, an owl, a camel. No, a mermaid, she decided. She would try a mermaid. Michael would approve.

All morning she wrestled with the wire, getting the dimensions just so. Then she waited for Daniel to go off at lunchtime before she found a patch of flattened grass, poured a bit of cement onto it, and repeated the process she had watched for days; powder, sand, water. She stirred it with a stick, round and round, until she had the perfect consistency. It *was* like making dough. Then she started packing the mixture around the frame. The cement burnt her hands, collected under her fingernails, but she waited till she was ready to leave the first batch – the base and the tail – to dry, before she went back indoors to find some kitchen gloves.

She was mixing the second lot when he returned, wiping his hands on his jeans, taking his own gloves from his pocket. She was aware of him shooting her a questioning glance, before he took the white bag back to his piece of tin, and started his own portion. She did not explain what she was doing. There was no point; she knew he would not be interested anyway. It was a relief to have something she wanted to do. A relief to be able to ignore him ignoring her.

She scraped and smoothed the mermaid's tail. Those she had seen at the Owl House in Nieu-Bethesda had tails decorated with chips of brightly coloured glass and mirrors. She wondered if it was still the same. She couldn't have been more than eleven or twelve when she visited there.

Her father had been commissioned to go to Nieu-Bethesda to fix the organ in the church. Damp, the rector had said. The organ was sticking because of damp.

They travel all day from Cape Town in the old red Mercedes, the two of them, stopping off at Beaufort West for a hamburger and strawberry milkshake at the Wimpy. They drive for miles through the Great Karoo – stark, mirage-like, the highway through it straight as a pole, each signpost an event. She remembers her father hitting the hooter now and again, to alert lazy birds on the road, the occasional tortoise in the brush alongside it, the sky above empty and endless, mirror to the desert.

Not long now, dear, he reassures her now and again. Look out for the turn-off. That's your job.

To pass the time, he tells her about the Owl House. About a woman called Helen Martins who lived there, all alone, making statues out of cement and crushed glass.

It's a sad story, he says.

Why? she asks.

Because it ends tragically. She killed herself. Drank caustic soda. Took three days to die.

Why did she do that?

She was old, she was sad, he explains. They say she was going blind, from all the crushed glass. Sometimes she put the glass on the ceiling, you see. I suppose it fell in her eyes now and again.

And with that, it finally comes, the signpost pointing to Nieu-Bethesda. They rattle and jolt along the corrugated road, through the dust and stones, and just when she thinks it is all a mirage, that they will never get there, they turn a corner. Below them, lush and treed, there it is, the church spire rising up from the middle. They drive along a road, unsure where to go, when suddenly she points to a wall.

It's there, she says. It's behind the wall.

What, dear? he says.

The Owl House. Helen Martins's house.

How would you know, then? he asks, following her directions anyway.

I don't know, I just do, she says.

And she's right. As he pulls up outside, on the dust road, a rickety sign says *Owl House, museum.*

Well, I'll be darned, he says. The girl's fey.

Can we go inside, Sam? she asks, opening the car door.

She does not remember how long they spend there. Only that each room remains etched in her body, in her cells, like DNA. The Cobra floor polish ceiling – the lid of the tin replicated exactly in crushed glass overhead. The elongated single bed, made specially for the married lover, Hattingh, whose baby Helen Martins aborted. The doll, made from fragments of cloth, to symbolise the child, strewn on the floor, the windows of stained glass. And the bath. In later years, the sombre stone bath would make her think of the Holocaust. A cleaning chamber designed for torture. Even as a child she can sense that the brightness of the Owl House, its terrible light, glinting from every surface, serves only to contrast the contorted shadows of its creator.

And then the courtyard. When she walks into the large expanse, she feels as though she had stepped into another dimension. She keeps looking behind her, to one side then the other, trying to catch whatever it is.

Because to her it feels as though each and every statue is moving. With their cement bodies, and glass eyes, they feel alive. To her it seems each one is haunted by the spirit of the woman who created them.

They stay for two nights in a rustic cottage in the main street. There are no real shops or restaurants, just a petrol station, a corner grocer and the church. The bells ring on the hour, waking her through the night. As she lies in the pitch dark, she wonders if it is Helen Martins ringing the bells. Helen Martins who still pervades every breath of that place.

This is how it is, she thinks. This is how it is with the spirits of women who leave behind what they love.

The minister of the church arrives the following morning while they are cooking their oats, to explain what happened to the organ. In broken English, and with a strong Afrikaans accent, he tells them that he is very angry about the organ, very angry. The reason that the organ has damp – *I mean, this is the desert, you know, damp is not something we worry over* – is due to a leak in the roof.

Her father nods politely and says it is understandable. But the minister says that this is not the point. The point is that he paid a great deal to have the roof repaired a few years before. A man – *a bliksem, from out of town, English* – had gone into the roof, worked for several days, then told him the roof was fixed. After the first storm, when it didn't leak, he sent an invoice, and was paid. *Not cheap. Daai bliksem was not cheap, sir.*

Her father nods, while the minister explains that the first year after the repairs was fine, even the second, but three years later there were some particularly heavy rains – *flash floods, you know* – and the roof started leaking like a sieve. *Like a sieve!*

Again her father nods while the minister, now leaning forward and growing a little pink, tells them that when they sent a labourer up into the roof to see what was wrong with the repair, he had come down and explained that directly beneath each leak, above the ceiling boards, were little buckets tied with string, and that these buckets were full. And that was how the organ had damp. Her father stares at the minister for a few seconds, then bursts out laughing. The minister looks surprised, then bursts out laughing too. And then they go off to look at the organ, and later have dinner with the minister and his family. The minister's daughter is a serious, solid girl, who shakes her hand when she meets her, and says *aangename kennis*. Prompted by her mother, the girl invites her to go and play in her bedroom after dinner. But Ana says *nee, dankie*, and sits alongside her father, who soon announces they must leave, they are a little tired, they were up early that morning. It is a well-meaning evening, he says to her on their way back. Awkward at first, particularly because of the language barrier, but soon eased with laughter and good intentions. When they drive back to Cape Town two days later, they agree that nobody really knew what the other one was saying.

It was the laughter that fixed it, says her father. Laughter, music of the breath.

She spent the rest of the afternoon building up the mermaid's torso. The mortar was harder to manage with gloves, but at least the skin on her palms had stopped stinging. She found herself humming as she worked, shaping the belly, the breasts, the shoulders. And quite suddenly she wanted to speak to Michael. Michael – who from the day they met had teased her that she was half mermaid.

She's barely fifteen, alone on the beach late one afternoon, on her way back from the shipwreck. She stops, wades out a few paces, then climbs a rock to watch a school of dolphins just beyond the shorebreak. Suddenly a face pops out of the water, a few seconds later the bright fin of a surfboard. Then it disappears, reappearing soon after, even closer to the rock.

Hello, says the face.

Hello, she replies, as he dips under the water again, porpoise-like in his black wetsuit.

Then he's off again. Next, she sees him lying on his board, legs splayed, paddling frantically with one arm, then swinging himself up and crouching before catching a wave.

Then again, circling on the board. Then up and going for the next wave, then the next. Then he hauls himself out of the water and plops himself next to her, dripping unapologetically all over her sarong. Even sitting, he towers over her.

Do you, he gasps. Do you live in a castle under the sea? In spite of the glare of the setting sun, she can see his very blue eyes, his broad smile.

No, she giggles. She can feel her cheeks burn.

Not even on weekends?

She shakes her head.

What's your name? he asks.

You first, she replies.

Neptune, he says. Then he's back in the water.

Come on, he says.

What are you doing? she asks, shrinking back.

Come on. Come and swim with me, mermaid. Take me to your castle.

It's cold, no . . . But she lets him take both her

hands and draw her in, in her sarong and strappy cotton top. An icy wave crashes over their heads. A baptism.

Come and watch me surf tomorrow, he says, after they stagger back, shivering, to the shoreline. Same time, okay? Small waves splash around her ankles, no hint of the currents just a few steps away. Then, still dripping and holding his surfboard under his arm, he drops his head and very quickly kisses the three freckles on her right shoulder.

She had read in some women's magazine in London that the pattern of a relationship is set in the first two weeks. When she cast her mind back over that fortnight, she couldn't help wondering if it were true. Her life with Michael so far had been exactly that – she was a willing and supportive audience, watching from a distance, from a rock where he had placed her, high enough for her to see and applaud everything, as he rode wave after wave; as he was elected Student Representative Council President, completed his degree with distinction, worked his way up at IFDA, won his way into the hearts of decision-makers and funders the world over.

In exchange he offered her sporadic adoration, and a voice, when she did not trust her own.

That day, you sitting on the rock, like a mermaid, he would say. That moment, looking up at you, sitting so neatly, your shoulders through your lovely hair, all fire and sun, your sarong fallen away to show your legs. That moment, I knew you were *the one*.

What if I hadn't been interested? she'd said.

Not possible, he'd said with a grin. Not possible for *the one* not to be interested.

Are you sure?

Absolutely. And besides, I'd have hunted you down

for ever. In the end you would have had to give in, just to get some peace.

So sure is he of their destiny as a couple that he never bothers to find out how she feels about it. So convinced is he, so certain for both of them, that she too never doubts it. Never doubts it at all. Not then.

And that is how it starts, that Christmas holiday, Michael just finishing high school. Every day they meet on the beach. Mostly he walks with his surfboard, from Kommetjie, where he stays. And on days when the surf is bad, he rides his bike over, and she joins him, cycling up Ou Kaapse Weg to Silvermine Nature Reserve, freewheeling all the way back.

You will be careful, won't you, her father says.

She doesn't really know what he means, but she nods anyway.

Aren't I always, Sam?

You're a good girl, her father nods. But his brow is still furrowed. Just . . . Just be careful, that's all.

Okay, she says. Don't worry, Sam. I'll be careful.

It is the break before Michael starts university. He has organised himself a job for the holiday – a runner for a film company – to earn some money before the term begins. During the weeks when they are shooting, he is up at four in the morning, finishing only after dark, sometimes working through the night. But as soon as he is free, he cycles over, sometimes showing up at ten in the evening.

The boy's really taken a shine to you, her father says.

Think so? she says.

Of course. Be a fool not to, wouldn't he then? Sam replies. Has he heard you play?

No. Not yet, she says.

Not? Why not?

Oh, I don't know. Maybe I don't know him well enough yet.

Good girl, her father says. There's plenty of time.

THIRTEEN

I'M MAKING A mermaid, she said when Michael
answered his mobile phone.

Why? he asked. And why do you sound so chirpy?

I don't know, she said. It reminded me of you. Of that
day we met. I wanted to tell you.

What else are you doing? he asked.

Getting the wall fixed, she said. Sorting things out.
Where are you?

Paris, he said. Some good meetings today. We're
setting up some phenomenal programmes.

That's good, she said. You sound inspired.

Yip. You know, if all goes according to plan, Africa
will be part of the Information Society by 2015.

Sounds expensive.

Yes, but there's massive funding. People seeing the big
picture. Leap-frogging infrastructure problems, straight
to other solutions – satellite, fibre optic cable, WIFI.

Thinking big, she said.

The only way, he said. Oh, and something else. I've
hooked up with some interesting new people in Paris. I
met them through Mikaela. She's a new intern, part-
time at the office. Swedish. A musician too, dying to
meet you. Anyway, these writers, poets, violinists all get
together once a week at different homes. Invited me
along.

You'd like it, he said, when she didn't respond. It's a really creative crowd. I think I've found our *tribe* at last. I'm going again tonight.

She didn't know why, but she suddenly felt drained.

Got to go, she said.

She struggled to understand why he was always drawn to this. It was not because it resonated with something inside him. He was not musical. It could only be because it was something other, something he could never quite access within. He did like music, this was true, but mostly pop or rock. Anything that ventured beyond the familiar he would tend to switch off. And he positively hated opera.

The last thing I need is to be screamed at by some neurotic Italian who sounds like she's just received a parking ticket, he said when she suggested they watch *La Traviata*.

And yet he seemed to find artists and activists compelling. Irresistible. She sighed. From the start, she'd never felt comfortable with Michael's friends.

I'm not a social animal, she'd said as a teenager, way back then.

You're a mammal, aren't you? he'd replied. Nothing as inconsequential as her opinion should stand in the way of a good argument.

Yes, she'd agreed.

Well, mammals like mammals. That's normal, he'd said. Plain biology.

She hadn't argued. Never explained that even at school, she'd hardly ever invited a friend home. And after primary school, had never accepted an invitation to a party. They'd continued to invite her – hoping that one day she might accept. But she never did. Preferred to be left alone. Her father hadn't queried it. Was too distracted to think about it. Besides, he would have been shocked, if he'd probed a little, to discover that it was largely the music that had isolated her. While other little girls had wanted to play with Barbies, Ana had wanted to play Beethoven. She had never liked dolls. Never seen the point. Found them rigid and plastic. If she thought a friend was important enough, she'd finally pluck up the courage to put on her reading glasses, take out the flute, and play a song for her. But the special friend had tended to grow bored listening to classical pieces and had inevitably wandered off in search of games and toys, leaving Ana alone, feeling silly. So she'd quietly given up on having playmates.

For many years, it seemed to her that it was only music that was truly dependable. Especially when she started winning competitions, passing each grade with distinction. It was then, in those brief moments of victory, that a light would flare up in her father's eyes. *She loved the flute, your mother. How she loved the flute.* But she couldn't sustain it. Couldn't keep the joy from slipping away from him again, try as she might.

At times when she was most honest, she knew that it was a relief to leave that weight behind when she left for England. Yet the relief was short-lived, the first guilt only to be replaced by the second; she had cost her father his bride, and then abandoned him too. A part of her felt she deserved her retribution, the slow and crippling understanding that music too could forsake her. That success in a city such as Cape Town did not guarantee success in a place like London, where the competition was so much more intense and appointments mostly went to those with stronger qualifications.

*

She had known Michael for several months before he found out about the flute. It happened by accident. She'd left it in the kitchen, and Michael, thinking it was in for repair, had picked it up and pressed his mouth to the lip plate.

No, not like that, she says automatically, taking it from him, and showing him how to position his lips to make a sound.

Can you play something? he asks. Do you play?

Now and then, she says, putting it back in the case.

No, don't put it away. I want to hear you play. Come on, Ana, please.

He is the first person in her age group to take an interest. And he looks so animated and enthusiastic that she finds it hard to refuse. So she takes out the music she's been practising, puts on her glasses, and runs through the piece once.

Wow, he says, when she's finished. That's incredible. You're so talented. Why didn't you tell me?

Soon after, their relationship becomes *official*. He tells his peers that he has a girlfriend – a musician. They want to meet her. There are invitations to parties, picnics, twenty-first birthdays. With the money he earns from the film company during the holidays, he buys himself the faded grey VW Beetle, and the two of them buzz around everywhere in it.

He boasts that the quality of the car is inversely proportional to the calibre of the sound system, turning up the volume on the tape deck – Yazoo: *Upstairs at Eric's* – till the windows vibrate.

Michael has a wide variety of friends, mostly students. She's still a schoolgirl. Still has two years to go before she starts her music degree. She knows the gap shows. The friends are kind to her, in an off-hand way, particularly when Michael introduces her as a musician, an artist, says she is *gifted*. And that she attended her first protest march in '76, at six years old after the Soweto riots. But when they learn her age, that she is still deep in high school, they assume that she won't share their interests as newly fledged opinion-makers in the grown-up world. And they are right. She doesn't care much for parties, politics, drunkenness, dope. She isn't interested in who is dating whom, or why. She finds the talk about protests on campus, police with tear gas, rubber bullets, arrests, rather frightening. And even though she tries her best, it is very clear to all that she simply has nothing to say.

Michael is patient, but she fears she embarrasses him. She lies awake at night, thinking, going over each event. She so wants him to be proud of her. In the end, she makes mental lists of topics of conversations she can raise with the group, before he picks her up. Sometimes she even scribbles ideas for things to chat about on a piece of paper and hides it in her pocket, or her purse, rushing into the bathroom to check she's covered it all. But mostly they aren't interested. And in the end he starts going to functions without her.

The only one from the crowd who asks after her is Willem Nel. The first year that she knows Michael, Willem Nel is just a name. A charged one at that; rumour has it that Willem Nel was in the clink for having killed a man. A policeman, someone says. Resisting arrest, says another. The story grows to such an extent – later including details of his tackling several armed policemen with his bare hands – that when he shows up at a party one evening, the crowd is amazed. And respectful. Willem Nel has pocked skin, hidden partially by five o'clock stubble, and dresses in old jeans and a leather jacket. He stands at the bar, pouring people drinks, and as the evening progresses notices her standing on her own. He jerks his head for her to join him. Pours her a whiskey. Pulls up a bar stool for her to sit alongside him. And that is the sum total of their interaction. Each time he is at a function, he looks out to see if she is on her own, while Michael mingles, smiles, fills spaces with a thousand words, to the beat of Carly Simon or Eddie Grant. Willem Nel usually takes a sip of whiskey while taking it all in, then glances across at her, motions for her to come and sit with him at the bar, finds her a seat, and then stares ahead, beating his fingers on the counter to the sound of the music, hour after hour, till Michael comes to take her home. This silent conversation with Willem Nel tends to be the most meaningful she'll have in that particular crowd.

On one such evening, the party is interrupted. She is seated next to Willem Nel at the makeshift bar, when three policemen arrive and, using loudspeakers, announce that the gathering is illegal. The officers then start throwing people randomly into their yellow van, until the vehicle is stuffed with drunken party-goers shouting and whistling. There is an air of jubilation, a charge of excitement that runs through the crowd like a live current, to the degree that those who cannot be transported in the police van voluntarily pile into their own cars and follow the van to the police station. Michael is one of them.

She sits very still, her chest thumping, hardly daring to breathe while the room empties out. After the last person jams themselves either into the van or one of the other cars, she turns and faces Willem Nel, who also has not moved for the duration of the event.

Just us, she says.

He nods. Hands her another whiskey. They sift through the cassettes. Change the music. Willem Nel chooses Thin Lizzy.

A few hours later, the party returns, thrown out of the cop shop with threats, warnings and *credibility*. Michael has almost forgotten she is there. She taps him on the shoulder, asks if they can go home now.

Yes, he replies, of course. Then he starts telling her all about it, talking all at once, the way he does when he's excited, all hands, eyebrows, shoulders.

It's only when she starts the music degree, giving recitals, having the odd review in the newspaper, that she feels his pride in her surge again. So when the army call-up comes when she is still halfway through her studies, it is in this spirit of confidence that they leave for London, sure that there she will find her wings.

Tonight, he had sounded different on the phone. Perhaps in Paris he was closer to it now, to finding the bohemian enclave he'd been searching for. And without her help, in the end. That would explain the buoyancy in his voice. The ever-so-slight shift. They were probably getting together, right now, his Paris crowd. She could imagine the low lights and laughter, glasses of wine, someone tuning instruments, music in the background. Michael at his most charming, towering and beaming, while she sat ten thousand kilometres away, in the orchestra of the dark, listening to the sea.

That night she dreamt of Paris. That she was back in the Jardin du Luxembourg, sitting near the grotto, watching the statue of *Acis et Galatée*, mesmerised as usual by its grace. Acis, the young shepherd so in love with the nymph, Galatea. In the dream it was she, not the gods, who wanted to warn them that such joy cannot last. That the giant Polyphemus, in bronze behind them, would end their happiness. In the dream, she tried to stand up, to point to the rock that the monster was holding, the rock that would crush Acis. But her limbs were liquid, her voice sleep-logged, words falling like dull river stones into the water.

FOURTEEN

THE MORTAR SHE used for the mermaid was acidic, bit into her hands, lodged itself under her fingernails. But she found the work exhilarating; giving form to the statue's shoulders and neck, extending the arms forwards, palms upwards, shaping and working each finger, smoothing and cladding. She was in no hurry to finish the project, allowed days to pass between, during which she'd dig around the garage for bits and pieces she may need: pieces of glass, or mirror, that would be useful to decorate the tail, the odd tile. She'd taken an old pestle and mortar from her father's workshop, and used it to break these up into pieces no larger than a deformed fifty-cent piece.

At one point, she noticed Franz walking through the long grass towards her. Daniel seemed to notice it too; immediately dropped what he was doing, took the wheelbarrow and headed for the river. Franz said he was waiting to go to a meeting, just wanted to see what was happening, stood around for a while, stared in the direction Daniel had gone, then shook his head and left.

She was relieved. She had started the mermaid's face, and wanted to concentrate. Kept it simple – a straight nose, hollows for the eye sockets, indications of long hair. When it had almost dried – the mortar dried quickly – she took a twig and dragged it through the hair several times, to show the wind. She had little time to get it right. She hadn't noticed Daniel leaving for lunch, or even his return. She had gone back to work on the eyes, following the example of Helen Martins's Owl House creatures. She'd already deliberately broken one of Franz's empty wine bottles to decorate the tail. She picked out two pieces and chipped away at the dark green glass until she had two eye-shaped pieces, and stuck them in. Suddenly the statue came alive. She stood back to look at her – the tail swirled round, encrusted with glass and small pieces of mirror, the flow of her waist up into her high breasts, shoulders and long neck, the arms outstretched, pleading. But in her eyes, resignation.

Hello, Helen, she said to the fishwoman.

He-nin! said a voice behind her.

She turned to find Daniel holding Tapiwa.

Can you look after her this afternoon? he asked. Angelina's busy.

Yes, she said. Let me go and wash my hands.

She found babysitting Tapiwa very easy. When she wasn't creating the mermaid, she would go over to the van der Veers' at least once or twice a week in the afternoons to help Angelina with her. The black woman welcomed the assistance, as she cooked, or polished brass, the radio going in the background. It was on one of these afternoons that Tapiwa stood up and, clutching the side of a chair, started bouncing her chubby legs and her double chin to the beat of the music. Up down, up down, her purple mouth gleaming with saliva.

Are you dancing, Tapiwa? said Angelina, smiling.

That's amazing, Ana said. She's dancing before she can walk.

Ja, she knows, said Angelina, turning up the radio. She knows that it is better to dance than to walk.

You think so?

Yebo. When there is rhythm there is no lies.

She smiled as the black woman started to move her head slightly to the song.

Angelina tapped her heart with her fist. First music you hear, your mother's heart.

Is that why black people wrap their babies to their backs? So that they can feel their mother's hearts?

Angelina laughed. Maybe, I don't know.

Tapiwa toppled over and started to gurgle. Ana propped her up on her jelly legs once again, so that she could bob up and down with the song.

My father used to say that the most important things are often the hardest to say, Ana said. He said that's why we have music.

Ja, said Angelina. Or poem, something like that. Or singing, dancing. Same.

Angelina was making Tapiwa some rooibos tea. Waiting for it to cool.

Sometimes it is a medicine for inside, the older woman continued. That's why, in some places in Africa, the word *artist*, is same like word for healer.

Tapiwa suddenly lost balance and sat down with a thud. For a moment it seemed she was going to cry, but then, in her low voice, she started to giggle. Ana reached down and reinstated Tapiwa on her wobbly legs.

What about toyi-toyi? she asked Angelina. That's another way to use dance.

Yebo, said Angelina, her voice less playful. But that is another story. They could control everything, but not the singing and the dancing.

Did you toyi-toyi?

Everybody toyi-toyi, said Angelina. Toyi-toyi is easy. The steps you make with your feet are same like drum. The big people, the small ones, in the schools, when you go to work, when you march. Because never you allowed to say anything wrong about the Government. Never you allowed to complain. That is why, if you don't toyi-toyi you go mad.

How come they didn't figure it out, that you were protesting when you were toyi-toyi-ing? Or did they?

We clever, said Angelina. If at a funeral, or having a meeting, or in the street, and the police they come, we change the words to church songs. She smiled. *Yebo.* Instead of Mandela, we say Jesus. And then they don't know what to do. Because they know, that is what we do. Black people, we sing. Singing is same for black people like talking for white people.

She handed Tapiwa the bottle of tea.

And then, she continued, shaking her head, sometimes they run for their guns, for tear gas, rubber bullets, water, all that stuff, anyway. Because when black people sing, the police, they get very scared.

She thought back to the protest march she'd found herself caught up in in Adderley Street after the Soweto riots. Her father rinsing the tear gas from her eyes.

Because the men with sticks were afraid.

Without Angelina, the child had only one requirement: that she could see Daniel. With this in place, she was placid. Quiet. Could crawl, stand and bounce, but mostly she lay on her back, or sat watching, staring out, now and again bouncing and gurgling Daniel's name. At certain points in the afternoon he would set aside his tools, pull off the gloves and come over to feed her. She didn't argue or spit it out. When he finished, he allowed

Ana to give her a bottle, which she would clutch and shake, before falling asleep.

But that afternoon, the baby seemed out of sorts. Unusually listless.

Come on, love, said Daniel, trying to coax her to eat.

She's usually so good about food, said Ana.

Come, baby, open mouth for Danny, he said, opening his own mouth to show her how.

Maybe she's not well, she said.

With that, Daniel stopped trying to feed her, packed up her things, and took her inside.

That evening, Franz arrived while she was carrying the mermaid, Helen, back to the courtyard.

Here, let me help you, he said, rushing towards her. You shouldn't be carrying things like this until your ribs heal.

The wind had grown wild, flinging his hair up, pushing the fabric of his clothes against his slightly bent frame. He placed the statue on a log, and went back to retrieve his parcels. The mermaid watched, her arms stretched forward, hands opening upwards, wistful.

Franz did not seem to notice. Dropped the bag with the bread and cheeses and wine on the kitchen table. The door banged shut.

What a day, he sighed, collapsing into a chair.

What happened? she asked.

Long story. I developed some houses in a township. Khayelitsha. Part of an organisation I belong to. Upliftment, you know. We're tied in and linked to all kinds of initiatives, but basically there's a small core of us who did the work.

And what's the problem?

The problem is that families moved into the houses, and have been there a couple of years already, without paying a cent rent. I've turned a blind eye, but the organisation wants to evict them.

Understandably.

Well, yes, I suppose so, he said, running his hand through his hair. It's just that last time something like this happened, there were death threats, mothers crying with babies strapped to their backs, all kinds of nonsense.

So why do you get involved in the first place? she asked.

He looked at her and sighed again. To help. To do the right thing. I don't know.

All these committees, organisations, she said. I mean, it's very noble. But why so many? What's behind it?

You mean, some kind of white guilt? he suggested.

Yes, she said. Any colour. I don't mind.

Aren't we all? he asked. Aren't we all guilty?

She remembered Angelina's comment, *All this helping people. It's not bring her back.*

After he left, braving the gale to walk home, the phone rang.

It's me, said Michael. He sounded warm.

Oh. I wasn't expecting . . . she said.

On your birthday? You didn't think I'd call?

My birthday? She gave a little laugh. Is it?

You're thirty, and you don't even realise it? A real grown-up now. Congratulations. And to celebrate, I have some good news. Last night, at this get-together I told you about, Mikaela told me something I didn't realise. She's a student at the Sorbonne, that's why she only works for us part-time. The rest of the time she studies music there. She told me that they have some foreign student programme, whereby they take students from other countries, classes are in English, and I thought . . . well, you know.

What?

I thought maybe you'd come back quicker if I arranged for you to study at the Sorbonne, finish your music degree, live here in Paris, not London.

She was silent.

Hello? he said. Are you there?

Yes, she replied.

So I called them up today, and it's true. They actually do that. I spoke to the professor about you. Told him how talented you are. Told him you were *gifted*, but had lost confidence somewhere along the way.

Why?

Why what?

Why did you tell them that?

Because I want you to be with me, he said, his voice suddenly small.

She could sense his mood shift. A window bangs in the wind upstairs in her father's workshop.

And what did they say?

They said they'd like to meet you. They're doing auditions at the beginning of the year. That's only a couple of months away. You could come over, we could take a bit of a holiday. Be together, in Paris again?

Oh, she said, sitting down.

So you're keen? Can I call the guy? Set it up?

Yes, okay.

Good.

And your project? How that coming along?

ICTs for Africa?

Yes. You sounded so excited about it.

It's going to change the world. Had some excellent meetings today. The United Nations are on board too.

Want to set up a meeting with us soon. Mikaela thinks she might be able to swing it that we have a conference in Moscow. Wouldn't that be exciting?

She sounds innovative.

She's extraordinary, he said. Brilliant. Speaks five different languages. Learned Italian just so that she could read Lorca in his original tongue.

He was Spanish.

Was he? A pause. Silly me. Must have been Pessoa, one of those.

You sound happy, she said.

I'm part of something that's going to help alleviate poverty, provide education, provide health solutions for HIV Aids and TB. I feel like I'm really making a difference to the whole African continent, it's quite a thrill.

It must be, she said. Just sounds a little too easy.

There'll be huge hurdles, naturally, he said. Bridging the *psychological* divide will probably be more difficult than sorting out the infrastructural challenges. But not everything has to be insurmountably difficult, Ana. There was an edge to his voice. Sometimes, things work. Even in South Africa. In fact, when it comes to ICTs I'm relieved to say that it's not a complete embarrassment. Compared with the rest of the continent, South Africa and Egypt are pretty far ahead of the game.

Well, that's good news.

He paused. You know, you really need to get out of there. Get some perspective. South Africa does that to you, I remember. Tends to suck you in, shows you the world through blinkers. Nothing ever seems possible when you're there. No wonder you have no confidence.

Me?

No, not just you. People in general. It's oppressive.

But, you've just said that sometimes things work. Besides, whatever your personal feeling, you can't deny that things are working here. You need to come back to see how things have changed, in a pretty short space of time.

That's what they said about Zimbabwe for the first few years after independence. That honeymoon sure came to a crashing halt.

Come on, Michael. We were on the brink of a revolution.

A revolution. I see. Nice emotive word, revolution.

He was growing heated.

We may have been spared a revolution, Ana, but have you any idea, *any idea*, how many people were killed in faction fighting, Inkatha and ANC, in Natal? Any idea how many people were killed on the flats, in the townships, burning tyres round thrown round their necks, shacks torched, people murdered in their homes? Even today. Look at the crime. It doesn't make the newspapers of course. Too boring and common-place these days to be *news*. But just look at the rape, the murder, the hijacking the poverty. And here we are, patting ourselves on the back and singing *Nkosi Sikele iAfrika*.

He gave a bitter laugh, then launched back in. Ja. God Bless Africa, look at us, peace-lovers that we are. A shining light to the universe. No revolution for us.

She took a deep breath. Michael the politician.

There are also positive things happening, she said.

I see. And how do you know this? How many newspapers, journal articles do you read? How many people of different colour do you speak to?

What's your point?

I'd just like to know how informed you are to make these sweeping utopian statements.

She was silent.

He sighed, then gave a little laugh. I thought so. You don't have a clue. Just like half of South Africa. A country of ostriches. It hasn't changed one bit in that respect. Look, I hope you're right. But my take on it is that by and large – from discussion forums, academics, people who actually know something – the blacks don't care much about the whites – understandably. Or the coloureds or the Indians – maybe less understandably. And many of the coloureds still long for the Nat Government and despise the blacks. And as for the whites, those that aren't longing for the good old days are so politically knees together, so anxious not to blow it racially, show their roots, that they aren't even real anymore. Scratch the surface, and you'll see.

You're inconsistent, she said.

What do you mean? he retorted.

At university you'd have been the first to call for a revolution. For these kinds of changes.

People mature, Ana, he said, with a sigh. Everybody knows that students are prone to be radical. That's their role. He was teaching her again. With exaggerated patience. Besides, at university I was interested in equal opportunity. Just as I am now. I can't help noticing – and there are others, educated people, who agree – that it's far easier to preach platitudes than do anything real. At least I'm doing something.

Your viewpoints may change a little, Michael, she said. If they are yours. They may even make sense. But your anger is the same. And it has nothing to do with the country.

He sighed again. So you think South Africa's a haven of safety, then? he said.

Not particularly, she replied. But I'm not convinced it's that different from other countries. People kill one another all over the world, don't they? Only in other countries the equipment is often better, more technologically advanced. In first world countries killing is simply far more efficient.

She didn't tell him that she'd finished the mermaid. That she'd looked after a black baby for the afternoon, had dinner with the neighbour again. That her ribs were finally healing, she could feel it. She didn't tell him that her growing opinion was that those who ask and live life's questions, as Shanti suggested, are often more interesting than those who are born apparently knowing all the answers. She didn't tell him much at all.

Instead, she said goodbye, went upstairs and tried unsuccessfully to fix the banging window. But the handle had come loose and refused to be secured. Even her attempt at tying it closed with string failed, the wind too determined to force it open. Eventually she went to bed. Lay awake listening to it banging in the wind. To the wooden floorboards contracting in the dark like gnarled fingers cracking their knuckles. To the voices that rose up from the spaces between.

FIFTEEN

Can I come too, Sam?

I'll be five minutes, dear. The car's jammed full of timber. I'd rather not take expensive wood out in this rain.

I want to come too.

I'll only be five minutes, he says. Then I'll be back with the gas, and we can have the pancakes. Besides, it's cold out. You stay indoors and look after Finbar O'Neill, and keep mixing the pancake batter, meanwhile.

No, she says.

No what, dear? He's picking up his car keys, making for the door.

Me too, she insists.

'Fraid not, he says, picking her up and seating her on the table alongside the large bowl. Sorry, Ana. There's just no space in the car. Next time.

Then he leaves and locks the back door behind him.

Me too! she shouts.

At the sound of the car engine starting up, she jumps off the table and tugs at the door handle. When it doesn't open, she beats the door as hard as she can. Then kicks it.

Ow!

She hops on one leg then bends to rub her foot. Then staggers across to the portrait of her mother.

He went without me, she says.

The faded face in the swirl of lines simply stares. *Just a sylph of a woman. A suggestion.*

He went without me, she insists.

She draws her face up to the portrait. The lines seem to fade further.

Speak, she says, grabbing the picture with both hands. Speak!

Her eyes blazing with uncried tears, she shakes the frame from its hook and flings it on the ground. At the sound of glass shattering she gives an exultant *There!* Then charges upstairs.

Ana, come out, he says.

No, she says.

Come on, he says. Come out from under there. I don't want to eat pancakes on my own.

Silence.

What's got into you, dear?

He kneels down by her bed, peers underneath. Can see her huddled in the corner.

I'm flipping them, he says.

What?

The pancakes.

Why?

Because that's the rules. Pancakes aren't proper, aren't respectable at all unless they're flipped.

Silence.

All right. I'm going downstairs now. When you feel like coming out, you let me know. He starts to straighten his legs.

Oh, and one other thing. He bends down again and squints into the black. Try not to take it out on your mother, dear. She can't fight back, you know.

She does too, she thinks. *She fights back every day.*

In the early hours the wind grew angrier, till it banged the loose window in the workshop so hard that the glass broke. She had just fallen asleep, but woke sharply as it shattered. Switched on the light, then tiptoed through the house, flicking the lights and checking each room before she realised what had happened. She thought she heard the sound of a car making its way up the van der Veers' driveway. Glanced at the wall clock and saw it was past three. Must be mistaken. Then she went back to bed.

Much later that morning the handyman she'd found advertised in the *False Bay Echo* arrived with a new pane of glass – he'd asked for the measurements – and set about fixing it. She watched with intent. Watched him dig out the jagged pieces of glass from the dry putty, then scrape it away from the window frame, before smearing a new batch into the recess, and pushing the pane up against it. She saw him dip his putty knife into a small honey jar of turps, knock some panel pins into the wooden frame to support the glass.

Looks easy enough, she said, thinking out loud.

Everything's easy when you know how, ma'am, he said. Then set about replacing the broken handle.

With the window restored, and the mermaid complete, she wasn't sure what to tackle next. It was still early, the wind down to a murmur, the morning clear as a singing bowl. She had finally decided to seat the mermaid on a tree stump at the back door, with her hands extended as though asking visitors for alms. The overgrown hydrangea nearby already wanted to touch her. She went into the kitchen to find some clippers and started to trim it. The garden had needed work, possibly a complete reinvention, since her arrival, plants growing wild, alien vegetation springing up all over, weeds and creepers running riot. Soon she had retrieved her father's tools from the garage, rummaged around in the kitchen drawers for rubbish bags, and set about taming it.

It had always been her father's job, the garden. She had found his gloves with the clippers, slowly put them on, felt shivers up and into her arms as she touched the fabric that had covered his square hands.

The previous night's conversation with Michael was still spinning in her head. His happiness that turned so quickly to rage. She couldn't help thinking that the country was always there, a good scapegoat when he needed something to blame. A convenient well in which to pour his anger. Then there was France – to study in Paris, live with him there – these were wildest dreams a while back. It was important to keep an open mind, she told herself as she dug into the earth. Shanti had suggested that she live the questions. That she didn't need to know everything right away. Although, it struck her that this time she was no longer even sure what the question was.

She'd been clipping back the plants for some time, when she realised that Daniel was unusually late. With a fat gloved finger she moved the fabric to read her watch; was almost ten o'clock. She glanced across in the direction from which he usually appeared, but there was no sign of him.

She continued to clear away the debris closest to the cottage, cramming it into bags and emptying it into the compost heap in the far corner of the property. Eventually, the sun began to soften, and she realised it was after four. She locked the tools in the garage, threw the gloves onto the bonnet of the car, then headed back to the house to the loft, to wait for Daniel to do the motorbike ride round his garden, now a late afternoon ritual, the dogs, the baby, the motorbike and the side-car.

For hours she waited, till eventually the sun went down. Strange, she kept thinking, returning to the window, time and again.

She was on her way down the wooden stairs, when she heard a knock, saw Franz letting himself in.

You should lock the door, he said. Especially after dark.

I do, mostly. Forgot today.

He was heavy, sat at the table, head in his hands.

A terrible thing's happened, he said.

She pressed her hand against her chest to stop the pounding.

What?

Tapiwa. Tapiwa died last night.

Died? But I was with her just yesterday, it's not possible . . . She felt like retching.

I suspect she may've been HIV positive.

What happened? And Daniel?

Daniel doesn't say a god-damn thing. Where the baby comes from, why he has it, whose it is, he won't tell. I told you, he's a nutcase.

What happened, Franz? What happened last night?

It turned out that Daniel had come to Franz in the middle of the night, and asked him to take them to hospital.

The first thing he's said to me since he's been back, said Franz.

Tapiwa had developed a raging fever, was limp. By the time the doctors examined her, put her on a drip, she'd slipped out of consciousness. They were waiting for her to bounce back – babies do – so that they could run a battery of tests, for meningitis, malaria. But she never did. She didn't have the fight in her, somehow. Daniel was still holding her, the drip in her arm, when she stopped breathing. The nursing sister checked her pulse and confirmed she had died.

It's unbelievable how quickly it all happened, said Franz. I had no idea . . .

What will he do? she asked.

I don't know. He wanted to take the body home with him. When the hospital said it was against the law, I thought he was going to hit someone. Eventually, he insisted they cremate her immediately, which after making us sign countless forms, and demanding a ridiculous sum of money, they agreed to. He took the ashes and went into the mountains. I haven't seen him since.

And Angelina?

Angelina is distraught. She's cried all day. But she's also stopped me every time I've set out to find Daniel.

Did she know Tapiwa was sick?

I don't know. If she did, she wouldn't tell me. She doesn't like to come between Daniel and me.

He sunk his face back into his hands. She took a bottle from the fridge. Something to do. As though the scuffle of her feet, the necessary action required to open it, would fill something, some baby-shaped void that words could not reach. She poured them both a glass of wine. In silence they sat and drank and breathed and stared. As he was leaving, he suddenly grabbed hold of her, pulled her towards him. She pushed against his chest, pushed him away.

You're upset, she said. We're all upset. Goodnight, Franz.

*

She rose from her bed, from where she had been lying in the dark, pitching and tossing like a lost ship, and slipped outdoors. She headed for the clump of arum lilies in the corner of the garden. Lay down alongside them, her belly and breasts against the cold grass, face turned to one side. Closed her eyes. The late November night was still. So still she imagined she could feel the yellow heat of the stars burning her skin, the pulse of the ocean in her neck and wrists. And full. Pregnant with insects and animals and trees, each one, the harmless and the deadly, communicating in their language of silence.

The earth. Silently spinning, falling, breaking, reforming each and every millionth of a second. The earth, whose conspiracy it is to give everything it has, to offer up itself and only itself, and all of itself. Then to take back, one at time, all it has given, every richness, every fragment, every follicle, folding it deep into the furnace of its heart, in a cold and perfect contract.

SIXTEEN

DANIEL DID NOT return the following week, or the week thereafter. Each day she worked in the garden, each day looking up, craning to hear his footfall. At the end of every afternoon, she resumed her position in the workshop, knowing full well that he would never drive the motorbike again, but hoping somehow to see him in the garden, striding across, pushing the wheelbarrow filled with rocks from the river.

But he never came. Only the night, creeping down over the mountain and across the sea. A cloud of darkness and fog that seeped into the bones. She never bothered to cook, wasn't hungry. At the end of the week she called Michael in London, in Paris, on his mobile, but all three telephones just rang. She sank into a bath instead, something womb-like about the water. For hours she lay there, now and then adding more hot water. Even Franz had stayed away that evening. Stayed at home, waiting for Daniel.

She had just released the plug when she thought she heard something. She stopped the water running out and listened. But there was nothing. She must have made a mistake, she thought. She took a towel from the rack, then heard it again. Yes, dogs barking. George and Clementine. Barking with glee the way they did when Daniel drove them around in the side-car. And yet there was no sound of the engine. With the towel wrapped around her she went into the workshop to see if she could see anything, but the barking seemed to be coming from the other side. From Angelina's quarters round the back. There was only one room in the cottage that looked out on that aspect of the van der Veers' property, and that was her father's. The room that she had kept firmly closed since her return.

She stood before the door for some time, the towel still wrapped around her, her breathing shallow. The dogs had stopped barking. There was probably nothing there. Nothing there at all. She started to walk away. Stopped. It need not take long, she figured, to run in, check the window, see if she could see anything, then out. Besides, it was dark – she wouldn't see anything in the room, and nobody could see her either. Better that way.

It opened easily. An oblique triangle of light from the rest of the house fell onto the floor, the corner of the bed. She tiptoed in. Stopped and listened, as though expecting a clue. Something more than the shudder of wind on the panes now and then, and her blood's drumbeat in her ears. The room smelled stuffy. She crossed over to the two windows and pushed them open, first the one, then the other, as wide as they would go. It was pitch black outside. She stared for a while, hoping her eyes would grow accustomed to the dark, that the new moon, delicate as a baby's nail-clipping, would lend some light. But she found she could not identify anything. Not even the outline of the trees closest to the cottage, let alone the van der Veers' property. Only the smell of kelp heavy in the air.

She decided to leave the windows open for a while. Turned to look at the door. Compared with the ink of night, the room suddenly seemed lighter; she could just make out the shape of a candle on his bedside table. She smiled; he must have been one of the few people on earth who truly resented electricity. Growing up, she often suspected it was only for her benefit that he had agreed to having it installed. Or maybe the candle was there for those times when the electricity failed. She rewound the towel around her chest, and picking up one or two items on the table – a box of pills, some Vicks sweets – found the matches.

The room sprang to life in the candlelight. She shivered. Jerked her head to the curtains billowing diaphanous in the breeze. The part of her that wanted to rush out of the door, jump through the window, followed close behind, as she slowly made her way around the room. It had hardly changed. His bed was made, the green mohair blanket, frail and folded at the bottom. She touched the pillows, pulled out a pair of pyjamas that had been placed beneath them. She lifted them to her face, brushed her cheek against them. The smell of flowers. Her father smelled of flowers.

She pulled the towel loose, let it fall to the floor, and pulled the pyjama top over her head. She could feel the hem lightly scuffing her thighs as she rolled up the sleeves. It's all so neat, she thought. So normal. *Why didn't you tell me, Sam?* Did a part of you wonder if it were true? Doesn't death always carry on its shoulder some element of disbelief? At the close of a good story, can we ever accept that it has finally ended?

She sat on the bed, then flopped over and sunk her head into the pillow. Or were you scared I'd stop it somehow? Or try to. Yes, that's it, isn't it? She said aloud, You *wanted* to go. And cancer was your ticket out. Journey back to her.

She saw herself tugging at the bolted kitchen door, no more than six, as she heard her father driving away. *Can I come too?* Remembers flinging her mother's portrait on the ground, the broken glass.

She lay curled on the bed for some time, breathing it all in. Only four months ago he had lain right here, in the dark, or perhaps in the candlelight, wearing these pyjamas, thinking his thoughts. Her legs started feeling a little cold. Instinctively she reached for the blanket and pulled it over her. Something fell to the floor. She leaned over and picked it up. In the flickering light she could make out a whistle or some kind of flute. Ah, an Indian bansuri, she thought. Made from bamboo. She lifted it to her mouth and blew into it. Almost weightless. There was so much about Indian music she did not know. Music at university had meant classical, what they called serious music. The rest – including Indian, Celtic, African and South American – was termed *anthropological*, and counted some five or ten per cent of the course.

She sat up on the bed, squashing the pillows up behind her for support, so that she could experiment. It was so light compared with her silver flute that it felt like a toy. Was it broken, Sam? She found herself wanting to know. Or did you just play it for fun? As she tested and held each note she noticed a fabric contraption on the wall, holding a range of Irish whistles and Indian flutes. There was an empty space for the bansuri. She took out each one and blew into it. Oh, look. Look – these are gorgeous. And the penny whistle! The breathiness of the little flutes seemed to make her fingers light. Finally, she pulled out the low whistle and took it with her to the window ledge, where she could smell the sea. She tested it first with a scale, adjusting her fingers to the holes; it was set in D.

Against the disciplined framework of the scale, she started to experiment. First with some tunes she knew by heart, adjusting her fingers and her breath to allow for the half tones, then testing the open holes to create quarter tones, eighth tones. As she played she felt the sounds vibrating through her fingers and with each breath emptying out, a fullness growing within. Was this the true meaning of the Afrikaans word for complete, *volledig*? Fullempty?

The more she allowed her hands to sing, bending the notes, finding the grace notes, rolling the whistle, the more haunting the music. She leaned into it, as different memories and sensations flooded each texture, each tone. Her father and the loneliness she had failed to fill. Michael before they left the country, before she let him down. And her mother. Her mother, whose ghost had wound itself around a void that had been the heaviest weight she had ever carried. Whose absence was a wound without healing. A guilt from which she could never be absolved. The more she played, the deeper this language, this language deeper than words, moved within her, bringing with every note a kaleidoscope of pictures. Sam, glasses halfway down his nose, singing and fixing a mandolin in his workshop. Sam, asking her to stir the soup while he grated the cheese and told her once again the story of Connla of the Fiery Hair. Sam, coming through to her bedroom in his pyjamas to switch on the light when she called out to him, half asleep after a bad dream. Then Michael, sliding down the sand dunes on torn-up cardboard boxes that they had foraged from behind the supermarket. Michael, threading string through cowries, breaking it off with his teeth, and tying them round her ankles. Michael, dripping and gyrating with cold after diving, hanging on to her for all the warmth he could get, before making a fire on the beach and cooking the crayfish he had taken from the sea. Playing beach bats in the summer, diving for the ball. The two of them cycling into Silvermine Nature Reserve one full moon night, huddling by the river and trying to acquire a taste for whiskey. Michael. Berating her for having had too much sun, after they'd spent the day kayaking at Simon's Town then fallen asleep on the beach. That evening, the arc of his shoulder gleaming with summer, his mouth a feather, a flame, against her sunburnt thighs. Michael teaching her to drive, laughing like mad when she shifted gears from fourth to first – *Man, Ana, can you believe it'll actually do that?* – as the VW Beetle sprang into the air. Michael coming back after being elected President of the SRC and saying that what he most wanted was his girlfriend and a surf. Michael in Paris, producing the red prayer candle, gift from Sainte Geneviève.

Yet as she savoured each sound that she teased out of the low whistle, it occurred to her that she was no longer playing someone else's melody, no longer obediently hitting the quavers and semiquavers according to somebody else's transcription, no longer using music as a séance to reach the dead, or as a passport to Michael's bohemian rhapsodies, but allowing the music to take its own lead, allowing the music to play her, pulling her deeper and deeper through currents of sorrow and joy, each note an atom of grief and elation, split and reunited into one artery of song. When she finally stopped playing, because her nose was too blocked, she knew that the tears, still wet on her cheeks, had paid some kind of tribute. As though an overflow of something had forced its way through the cracks, the scars.

It is fullness that breaks us, as much as loss, she thought.

Returning to the room after blowing her nose, she noticed that the sounds of darkness seemed more acute. The shrill of crickets, occasional burp of a frog, the swirl of the ocean. And through it all, a beat. Was that possible? She leaned out of the window. Yes, someone was playing the drums. She waited a while, then lifted the whistle and started again, softly, so that she could still hear it. Her eyes were closed. She inhaled the night air once more, heavy with sea odours, seaweed and iodine. She waited to feel the beat move into her body, so that she could weave the music through the thud, thud, thud. It's primal, this sound, she thought, *elemental*, each note rising and falling, fluid then forgotten, pulsing with the rhythm and fire of the earth, before dissolving like salt into the gusts and twists of the sea.

She never knew how long they played that night. Only that at the end of it all, she thought she heard, but she wasn't sure, the heave and choke of a man who wept.

SEVENTEEN

I MEAN REALLY, Ana, it's ridiculous.

(Michael. The country.)

Where did you read that, Michael?

On Expat. It's true. The South African Police Force are spending thousands, maybe millions on security companies to keep them safe. To keep *them* safe. You gotta love it. It's a joke!

Michael was one of the editors of a website called expatSA.com. The site was a vibrant meeting spot of thousands of people who had left South Africa and were now living in various corners of the globe. It boasted a variety of topics varying from sport to recipes and places to find and/or order Milo, biltong, Mrs Ball's chutney. It even had a Lonely Hearts section. Michael sometimes called and read them to her for a laugh.

Thirty-something SA bachelor now living in Earls Court, seeks attractive female companion, 20–25, preferably blonde, for long-term relationship and shared interest in sport. Must have tickets to Saturday's England/SA game at Twickenham. Please send photo of tickets.

But the biggest drawcard the site had to offer was its discussion forum and letters pages. She had noted that seldom was there a faultline – any aspect of being South African that was not working – that did not reverberate with opinions as issues surrounding it were moved from the mundane to the ludicrous.

What's your point? she said.

The point is I'm not happy about you being there. You've been mugged already. You've been there since August. It's now December. You've had plenty of time to tie things up, whatever that means. What more are you waiting for?

I could have been mugged anywhere, she said. But I'll come over to Paris for the interview, all right? It's not that long to wait.

He sighed. She could hear him blowing his nose.

Besides, she added. You can't trust everything you read on the Internet.

Naturally, he said. But who would go to all the trouble to make up something like that?

I don't know, she said. An ex-pat?

We've got better things to do, he retorted.

How's the ICT project? she asked.

Good, he replied. Coughing.

I've been thinking about it, she said. Are you sick? I've been wondering how people in far flung places are going to use computers when they can't even read?

Touchscreen technology, he said. Just a cold or something. Can't seem to shake it off. Tele-kiosks everywhere, fully equipped with Internet, fax . . .

Bill Gates in Africa, she smiled. Think it'll work?

Actually, Bill Gates *is* making a big contribution.

She giggled.

What's funny? he said. Irritated.

I suppose he wants people to think that's philanthropic, she said.

Yes, he sighed. It's not without its challenges, this project, but it's the only way.

For what? she said.

For Africa not to be left behind in the digital divide, he explained.

She smiled to herself. This was Michael's favourite thing. To *teach* her.

Aren't they scared of . . . of being colonised, in a way, again? she asked

Yes, of course, he said. But it's also a way for Africa to *keep* its identity. Its cultural heritage. ICT – the Internet especially – is a perfect way to archive indigenous information.

And have it plundered by everybody else, she pointed out.

Silence.

Then, You're incredibly negative, Ana. And cynical for some reason. He sighed. I've been very patient, you know. I'm assuming it's the loss of your father, and this is just a stage you're going through, but I must tell you, I'm finding it very taxing.

EIGHTEEN

FOR THE FIRST time in years, she overslept. Daniel was already working, slowly mixing mortar, by the time she stepped into the garden. She wondered if it was her imagination, but he seemed thinner, older, turning the mixture with a stick, round and round. He did not seem to see her and she did not mind. Busied herself with trimming the pathway. She had found some lavender seedlings at the back of the house and was about to start digging small fissures when he called out.

Compost.

What? She jumped. For a split second she thought she'd misheard.

You'll need compost, he said.

I haven't turned the compost heap yet. It's a bit of a project.

She continued to dig, then placed the scrawny roots into each hole, fluffing them up with loose soil.

At midday he left, his hand on his lower back as he walked. She started on some weeding. On his return, he came carrying a large bag. She winced at the memory of him bringing Tapiwa, watched him make his way towards her, flopping the bag at her feet. A pungent odour flared up almost immediately. She jerked back.

Chicken manure, he said. It's strong. You only need a little.

Thank you, she replied, tucking her hair behind her ear, then watching him walk towards the wheelbarrow and head for the river.

She snipped off the corner of the bag with the clippers. Poured small heaps of the acrid mass around the new plants, then worked it in with a trowel, trying not to breathe.

There you are, she said to the seedlings. Then went to attach the hose-pipe.

You're very distracted this evening, Franz said, as she moved around the kitchen.

Hmm? she said. She was trimming a small bunch of flowers she'd gathered from the garden, arranging them in a tin.

I said you're very distracted. Is everything all right?

Sorry? she asked again, opening the fridge door and putting the flowers inside. Then turned to him, her eyebrows raised in question.

You've just put the flowers in the fridge, he pointed out. Is that what you intended?

Oh, goodness, no, she said, quickly retrieving them. Sorry. I'm a bit distracted.

He sighed. Ran a hand through his hair. That's what I said. Is everything all right?

Oh, yes. Everything's fine, she said. What can I get you to drink?

What about . . . what about your marriage?

My marriage? she said, confused. What about it? She sat down, forgetting about the drinks.

Well, doesn't your husband . . . what's the story there now? Are you separated?

No. No, of course not, she said. Why do you ask?

Just curious, he said.

I'll go to Paris in February, she said. To see him. She did not mention the audition. I should give him a call, she said, more to herself. He wasn't that well when I last spoke to him.

And then?

And then, she replied, automatically. And then I suppose I'll do what comes next.

Daniel's back, he said. Doesn't say a word. Angelina just cries. It's lovely.

And the eviction?

Still dragging on. I've issued the directive to go ahead. Waiting for the fallout.

After Franz had left, she gave Michael a call. He'd been sleeping.

Hello, baby, he croaked.

You sound awful.

Didn't go to work today. He started to cough.

Michael, I think you should see a doctor, she said. Please, there's been enough illness lately. Will you see a doctor? Tomorrow?

Okay, he said. He sounded soft. Warm. It's just flu, though. I'll be fine.

Still, she said. You will see a doctor, won't you?

Yes, little one, he wheezed. Don't worry. I'll see a doctor.

She sat on her bed and stared at the floor. She felt guilty that Michael was sick, so far away. Guilty because she was not there for him, to help him, cook for him – *in sickness and in health* – and a deeper guilt, because there was a part of her that liked it. Liked the fact that he needed her, wanted her, was warm and familiar and fluid; not Michael the Omnipotent, full of angles and clever quips, each day selling another piece of his carefree soul for a cause.

But you're not, she said to herself. You're not there, you're here. In a parallel universe, different cadence, different hemisphere. She climbed the stairs to her bedroom and lit the small prayer candle from St Geneviève. For Michael, for his healing, for the shared storylines that ran deep across their hands.

A while later she softly blew it out, stood up and wandered into her father's bedroom. She'd left the door slightly ajar, left the whistle and the bansuri on his bed, ready to pick up and play. She lifted it to her mouth and blew into it, moving her fingers over the holes to test the sounds. Again, she tinkered until she found the flow, holding each note until the next one presented itself, moving from slow to fast, then back to slow, each note filling, emptying, like the sea. She stopped and listened. Could hear it in the distance, the great surge of the ocean, now and then a large wave bellyflopping on the beach. She listened as wave after wave shattered on the shore, seeing in her mind's eye imprints of the moon's longing shrinking from the sand.

She moved to the window and opened it as far as it would go, to invite the sounds in, the ring of the crickets, tree frogs, rush of the wind, and again, the distant sound of a drum, slow and sure as a death march. Then she lifted the bansuri to her mouth once more, and once more they played, with the ensemble of the night, to the breath and beat of the earth.

NINETEEN

SHE WOKE THE next day with a tune in her head. Was it her head? she wondered. Or her heart? Why not some other part, if an idea really needed to be housed within the confines of the body. Why not a song in her spleen, her liver, her solar plexus, like indigestion? Why not her arms? She liked that. She had woken with a song in her arms. It was something you could pull towards you and inhale, like holding Tapiwa, like holding a baby, something warm and changing and alive, full of possibilities – delight, heartbreak. She sank back into the blankets and smiled.

The melody was unlike anything she'd heard before. It was her own. She worked on it at night, at first playing the outline, stretching it out like a washing line on which she hung every note. With each new day she would hear another dimension to it. Each night she went back and worked on it some more, spinning and weaving its nuances into the tempo, breathing it into the light. It became the call from which he'd answer, a distant drumming, a dance.

The summer days flowed forward like a slow river. Flowers, mouthwarm to the sun, yawned and napped in the heat of the day while she worked on the back garden, creating pathways, an area for herbs, a small pond. A squadron of tadpoles was already shooting across it in tiny pliés and now and then birds dropped in to bath. The year turned. Her arms and legs grew more tanned, muscular, as her ribs healed and she was able to carry and move things around without discomfort.

Michael had recovered, or so it seemed. Aside from a flaming argument about her not being home for Christmas, he seemed to have relaxed. Her appointment with the Sorbonne had been confirmed for early February. Then one day he called from his mobile to say he was in hospital.

What happened? she asked. She felt her limbs go numb. I thought you were better?

So did I, he said. His voice sounded thin. But then I had some kind of relapse. They're doing tests.

When will you know?

I don't know. I'll phone you.

What do they think it is? Have they said anything?

They say it could be a few things, but they can't be sure till they get the bloodwork back, check the X-rays.

Will you let me know as soon as they tell you?

Of course.

As *soon* as they tell you, she repeated.

She tried to call later, but the phone was switched off, and remained so till the following afternoon. She paced up and down the house, now and then lighting the small candle and muttering. *Why didn't he answer?* When she finally got through, he sounded much better.

Pneumonia, he said proudly. But I'm through the worst.

Pneumonia. How did that happen? And the flu you had before that? Was that part of it? she asked.

Probably related. It's been very cold. But I'm on a drip. And on the mend.

How are you feeling now? Shall I come over?

A pause. Then, No, he said. It's a waste of money, considering you come to Paris for your interview soon. I'm much better.

Are you sure?

Oh yes, he said. I just sleep all the time anyway. I'll see you next month. Can't wait.

It's not long now, I suppose, she said. I've been worried.

I'll be fine, he said. But she could hear he was pleased. You know, Ana, he continued, while I've been lying here ill, I've been doing a lot of thinking.

And?

And I want us to stop fighting. We never used to.

I don't want to fight either, she said.

All I could think of was that if I were dying, you'd be the one I'd want around.

You're not going to die, she said hurriedly. And I'll be there in a month. Then if it all works out, I'll come back straightaway and sell the house.

You're a good kid, he said.

TWENTY

THE HERB GARDEN needed something in the middle. She tried seating the mermaid on a log and placing it at the centre, amidst the quadrants of basil, rosemary, fennel and oregano, but it didn't feel right. The mermaid wanted to sit on her tree stump at the entrance to the back door. She moved her back there. Stood staring at the empty spot, pondering. Another sculpture? A water feature?

A sundial?

It was Daniel.

Since she had been attacked she responded rather sharply to the unannounced presence of people. But she did not jump. She had a sense of him, his leaving with the wheelbarrow, returning, carrying cement.

You know how to make one? he said.

No. Do you?

I have a book somewhere. If you like, I'll ask Angelina. I made one when I was a child.

Cement? she asked.

If you like. Would you like to give it a try?

She stood back and had another look. A sundial might be perfect – just tall enough to hold attention. She could plant some annuals around it.

Why not? she said.

Angelina could not find the book. Told Daniel to

suka! when he asked her to look a third time. But Ana didn't mind. Started working on a wire frame anyway. Daniel continued with the wall. He was working some way up the property now, closer to the mountains, strengthening the retaining wall up against the banks. Although she seldom looked up, or scanned the horizon for his shadow, she found she knew his arrival, his movements instinctually. As though the flying insects conspired with the wind to tear something from him, a droplet of sweat or an eyelash, and bring it to her.

It was growing dark when he walked over to see how far she had come. She was packing up the tools. He sat on the same rock she'd found when she'd offered to help with the wall.

I'm going to plant giant Russian sunflowers around the sundial, once it's in place, she said.

Not something indigenous?

Most of the garden is indigenous. But I'm not completely botanically xenophobic. Now and then I plant something else.

He nodded.

Just then a shadow fell across her shoulder. She looked up and saw Franz standing slightly stooped staring at the two of them. Daniel did not move.

Will we be having supper later? Franz asked, staring at her, eyes like bullets.

She shrugged, then nodded. Sure, she replied.

See you later then? About an hour? His voice was clipped.

Yes. I suppose so.

He walked away.

What were we saying? she said to Daniel.

Botanically xenophobic, he replied.

Oh, yes. I just think a sundial needs, well, sun*flowers*.

And they have to be Russian? he asked.

I don't think they know they're Russian, she said, smiling. Nor do the other plants. No more than we know we're South African.

Meaning? he asked.

Well, do you know what it means to be South African? People say they're South African because of their roots, or their hearts. You know, the ones whose ancestors were killed in Anglo-Boer wars, or in Zulu wars, as though family blood in the soil gives entitlement. But I don't really know what all of that means, anymore, do you?

Nope, he said. But perhaps it's bigger than that?

She looked up.

I don't know, he continued but seems to me we're missing a trick if we spend all our time arguing about who has a right to be here and who doesn't, who belongs and who must leave. Isn't it more about getting to grips with the business of being African? Issues of belonging seem almost indulgent compared with Aids, poverty, illiteracy.

But how do we *know* if we're African? she asked.

Good question.

I don't know about you, she said. But I was born here, so was my mother, but my forebears are all European. Irish, Portuguese, even some Dutch.

Welcome to the human race, he said. Sounds like you're pretty much as mixed as most of the world. And even the Irish and the Portuguese and the Dutch might have started out at some other part of the globe. And the Queen of England is really German, and we probably all come from the same place anyway, the sea – though don't tell the fundamentalists that – and the only thing we can be half sure of, they say, is that Adam and Eve weren't Chinese, otherwise they'd probably have eaten the snake, not the apple.

She gave a little laugh. But it's a thought, isn't it, she mused. Do you belong in a place just because you were born there, or love it? Does the soul have a passport? Or do you simply pick the branch of the family tree that you prefer, with its preferred location, and hang your history on it?

I don't know, he said. I suppose there are those who feel more entitled than others, those who feel they have Africa in their blood, in their roots, a bit like your indigenous plants. Then there are those like the oaks and the syringa trees, planted here from afar, rooted here for centuries, flowering with beauty but fundamentally alien. He sighed. But in some ways, maybe we're all mongrels. Rain dogs, like the song. Our instincts washed away, some by blood, some by guilt, some by fear, a long time ago, running and running, never stopping, trying to find some sense of belonging, to pinpoint some little spot on the map, some place we can call home.

He stood up and stretched. Anyway. See you tomorrow.

Yes, she nodded.

Oh, and . . .

Yes?

Enjoy your supper.

She could not see his face. He was already walking away.

As soon as she had packed the tools away and returned to the cottage, she called Michael.

Much better, he said. Checking out of the hospital tomorrow morning.

She exhaled.

Had a huge bunch of flowers from IFDA, he said. Mikaela brought them round herself.

What kind? she said.

What kind of what?

What kind of flowers? she asked.

Flowers? Oh, all sorts. Red ones, orange, purple.

She smiled. That's good, Michael, she said. I like flowers too.

She was still talking to him when Franz arrived. Early. He looked clean-shaven. Sharp. She ended the conversation and headed for the kitchen where he was standing. She washed her hands in the sink and wiped them on the dish towel, before starting to chop and trim vegetables and chicken thighs for a green chicken curry.

So how is your husband? he asked, sitting down.

Actually he's been ill, she said. But thankfully he's on the mend.

Shouldn't you be with him? he asked.

She did not reply.

Sorry, it's none of my business, I know. I just can't see why you're messing around in the garden when you're needed elsewhere.

She sliced her finger. Excused herself and headed for the bathroom. Sat on the edge of the bath and ran cold water over the cut, water and blood flowing down the drain. Then wrapped a bandage around it and returned to the kitchen. He was pouring himself a glass of wine.

And what does Daniel have to say for himself? he sneered.

Nothing, really, she replied.

Didn't look like that to me. Looked like the two of you were having a pretty good conversation. I didn't think he was capable of one. He's become so . . . primitive.

She opened a tin of coconut milk, pulled the stems off the coriander, diced a chilli, popped a cashew in her mouth.

Enough about the garden, she said. May I have a glass of wine?

TWENTY-ONE

HERE, SAID DANIEL a few days later, handing her a narrow, triangular piece of rock. For the gnomon.

The *what?* She was pressing down on the wet mortar with an old tray, working on the face of the sundial, to make sure it was quite flat. Had not seem him approaching.

The gnomon. The thing that casts the shadow, so that you can tell the time.

Perfect, she said, taking it and pressing it in, holding it for a few moments while it set. Thank you.

By noon it was finished, the edges neatly trimmed with a trowel, the gnomon secure. She placed it in the centre of the herb garden and positioned it so that she could find the shortest shadow. She planned to check where the shadow fell every two hours so that she could mark it off.

Later that afternoon she was digging the ground around the sundial when he arrived carrying another bag of cement on his shoulder. She had been digging first with a fork, to loosen it, to crack open the tightly packed soil so that she could feed it, water it, soften it for planting. The seedlings for the giant Russian sunflowers were propped up against the wall, waiting patiently for their new home.

Looks good, he said, nodding at the sundial. Have you finished, or can you use this?

Not at the moment, she said. It's almost done. Thanks anyway.

Okay, he said, starting to walk away.

Daniel. She stood up, leaned against the fork and cleared her throat.

Yes?

Wait. Wait a moment.

He paused. What is it?

I'm leaving soon. I have to go to Paris for a week.

Oh, he said. How lovely.

Yes, she replied. My . . . my husband lives there much of the time.

He nodded.

I'm going for an audition.

He nodded again, the bag of cement still perched on his shoulder.

Do you want to go? he asked.

He's been ill, she said. I should have gone earlier. He said . . . he said he's realised that if he were dying, he would want me there.

If he were dying, he repeated, half to himself, nodding his head slowly, digesting each word. If he were dying he would want you there?

Then he lifted the cement off his left shoulder and heaved it up and onto the other one.

But enough about dying. Isn't living the thing?

TWENTY-TWO

Ana, he said.

Michael?

You didn't recognise my voice? Through his pretended reproach, he sounded amused.

Just haven't heard you sounding this well in ages, she said.

Thank you, sweetie, he said. I'm completely recovered. Now listen, there's a problem.

Her heart sank.

You there? Hello? he said.

Yes.

Mikaela's arranged for us to attend this big conference – I'm a key speaker – with the UN and all the major players. In Moscow. I did tell you about it, remember?

Yes. She knew what was coming.

And, unfortunately, it's quite soon. I didn't realise, being ill and all.

Yes, she said.

And, he sighed. And it's at the time of your audition in Paris.

I see.

So . . . *please* don't be angry. This is a big opportunity for me. I've been working towards this, we all have, all year. You must understand . . .

Yes, she said. I understand.

But I've organised everything for you in Paris. You won't have to worry about anything. Just go straight to the hotel.

Hotel? I thought I'd be staying in the loft?

No. They will be renovating or something then. Fumigating, I think. So I've booked you in at our special hotel. Hôtel de l'Espoir. I thought you'd like that.

Okay.

You don't sound happy. You loved that hotel when we stayed there before. I thought it would be a treat. I've paid for everything for the whole week. It's all sorted.

The sun had almost slipped into the sea when she arrived at Shanti's house in Scarborough. She had cycled all the way, through Kommetjie, along Misty Cliffs, with its white beach and net of spray, hoping that Shanti could take her and the rusty bicycle back in her faded bakkie. She had ridden hard and fast, counting on the exercise to knock it out of her. Her surging frustration with those with wings on their tongues, who made promises that flew out of their minds as soon as they mentioned them.

The structure of Shanti's house was singularly unexceptional. Yellow face brick, steel window frames, an old meranti-veneer door, chipped at the corners, plastic tiles in the kitchen, peeling up at the edges. Yet over the years, Shanti had woven herself through it, given it a glow. It was only two houses away from the beach, the sandy soil supporting an effusive bougainvillea – orange – that spilled extravagantly onto the stoep where some deckchairs sprawled. As she propped the bike up against the wall, she caught a quick glimpse of the purple velvet couches and colourful rugs inside the lounge. She knocked.

It's open, flower, called Shanti. Make yourself at home, I won't be a minute.

Ana sank back into the sofa, pulling an appliquéd cushion towards her and hugging it. The furniture and carpets were worn and moth-eaten in places, yet all Shanti's years seemed stored in their warp and weft. It struck her that occasionally a house has an aura of *home* that no interior designer could ever achieve no matter what the budget. Occasionally a house, even an ugly one, has a soul.

A rainbow filtered through the crystal hanging in the window, pulling her focus towards a squat candle holder in the shape of a large woman with enormous breasts. The woman had long silver hair and silver nipples. From the verandah the low moan of wooden wind chimes wafted through the sound of the sea, and in the window a thread of smoke rose from the incense.

She'd first cycled to Shanti's many years ago, just touching teenage-hood. She remembered finding the telephone number in her father's leather address book, and calling to make the appointment.

Is it a cleansing you're after, sweetheart? Shanti says.

No, she whispers into the phone. I need to talk to you.

She has terrible stomach pains, noticed some stains in her underwear. She's vaguely heard about the processes a woman's body goes through in her biology classes, but she isn't a woman. She's just a girl. And if she dies, what on earth will happen to her father?

Shanti gives her directions and she cycles all the way.

I think I'm ill, she tells Shanti, giving her the symptoms.

Oh, honey, you've got your period, that's all, Shanti says. Come, let me explain.

And she makes them both a mug of chamomile tea, and with some sketchy diagrams and clear explanations, tells her what she can expect and how often. Then she throws the bike in the back of her bakkie, and takes Ana home, armed with a supply of sanitary towels, tampons, a hot water bottle and a small bottle of lavender oil to dot onto her pillow at night for the headaches. She gives her a call the following day to check how she is getting along.

Don't be a stranger, sweetheart, she says. I'm here whenever you need me.

But that was many years ago.

Shanti appeared in a kimono, her hair wrapped in a towel.

Hello, flower, she said, holding out her arms. Oh, it's so good to see you, I'm so glad you came by.

As usual, the scent of her lingered long after she'd released her. Lemongrassy.

Here, pour us some wine, said Shanti, switching on the CD player and turning it down low, allowing Cesaria Evora to flow into the late afternoon. In the fridge.

Then she rubbed her hair with the towel and threw it over the corner of the door. Won't be a sec, she said, disappearing into another room, while Ana found the bottle in the fridge. She was staring at the label, it was called *Live-a-Little, Wicked Little White* and sported a painting of an overweight woman flying, when Shanti reappeared, her long honey-blonde hair combed and hanging in supple lines. She noticed the few strands of grey and white around her temples.

It's organic, said Shanti. Not bad.

How are you, Shanti?

I'm good, Shanti replied.

It's funny, Ana said. I never really believe people when they say that. I suppose it's because I don't often mean it myself. But you say *I'm good* in such a way that I believe you.

It comes from my cells, said Shanti. Besides, you vibrate at such a high frequency yourself that you'd pick it up if it weren't true. She threw a cushion on the floor in front of her and pointed to it. Come, flower, you sit right here, you look a little tight in the shoulders, let me fix it for you.

She dropped onto the cushion and crossed her legs, tilting her head as Shanti's firm hands worked her muscles. With Shanti, she found it as easy to move into silence as it was to talk.

Did you cut your hair, love? Shanti asked.

Yes, she answered. A few months ago already, when I came back. I did it myself.

Such pretty hair, said Shanti. Hmmm. It's a little skew at the back, it's always a thing to do it yourself, mind if I straighten it for you?

I'd like that, she said.

Just then the phone rang.

Back in a mo, said Shanti, picking up the receiver and asking the person on the other end if they'd call again a little later.

That was Adam, she said, settling back into the couch, wedging her knees on either side of Ana's shoulders. He's a sweet boy. I met him on the Inca trail many years ago. Still calls.

It was strange for her to imagine how Shanti's life had been since she'd stopped coming to the cottage. Strange to imagine her as part of other people's lives, other men.

To her, Shanti had always stayed fixed in her memory, a fairy in her kitchen more than twenty years ago.

Do you have a boyfriend, Shanti? she asked.

I have some people who are . . . special, said Shanti.

Not one specific one then? she said.

No, not really, said Shanti.

She felt a strange sense of relief. Felt the tightness in her shoulders start to give.

Why do you ask, flower?

I don't know. Just being quizzy, I suppose. I shouldn't pry.

You can ask whatever you like, said Shanti. I don't really do secrets.

They fell into silence again.

See, said Shanti, after some thought, I'm the type who can't really make promises to anybody unless I've got the mad crazies. And that's only happened once or twice. She lifted her hand from Ana's shoulder, took a gulp of wine, then pressed on with the massage.

Mad crazies? said Ana.

Yes. You know, the wild stuff. The kind that possesses you, wakes you in the night, shakes you into another reality.

And it happened once or twice? said Ana.

Yes. Thank goodness. Can't happen too often. And I'm so glad it did. Because it taught me something important. That if you have to ask yourself if you're in love, then you're not. It's that simple.

Hmmm, said Ana, biting her lip.

Really, flower. We overcomplicate things. Life is simple if we listen to our hearts. Stop trying to talk ourselves into things.

Ana was silent. Then after a while she whispered, What was he like?

What was he . . .? Suddenly Shanti stopped. Oh, baby. You thought I was talking about Sam, didn't you?

Ana swallowed.

You know, between us girls, I think I could have had the mad crazies for Sam Delaney. He was just the kindest man I ever met.

So . . . it wasn't him?

Sweetheart, beautiful as your father was, in *every* way, there was just no getting near that man. He operated in another reality.

What do you mean? she said. But she knew the answer.

He only had eyes for a ghost. Only one woman for him in this lifetime. And you, of course. Part of the reason I had such a shine for him was the way he was with you. It was poetry, watching the two of you. But there wasn't any space for me, so I got myself out before I found myself stuck with the mad crazies, and no place to go.

Shanti squeezed out from behind her and lit another stick of incense.

Sandalwood, she said. Isn't it gorgeous? Then she took a pair of scissors from a drawer and a fresh towel from the bathroom and set about straightening Ana's hair. There was a knock at the door. Shanti got up again and opened the door.

Oh, yes, okay, she said, handing a plastic bag to three urchins.

Bergie kids, she said. They're always here.

So, will you tell me about him? Ana asked, her chin tucked in as Shanti settled herself down again and started snipping away. About the other one. Not my father.

Oh, said Shanti, and sighed. He was special. And

important. He taught me a great deal. But the relationship ran its course. As they do.

Was it painful, moving on?

Yes, of course. And a bit confusing at the time. It turned out that he was a bit of a cad, had women in every city. She laughed. Which was quite a feat, because he also had a wife.

Did you know? she said. That he had a wife?

Yes, said Shanti. That I knew.

Didn't you feel guilty?

No. Why? I was in my truth. I'd feel guilty if I weren't. Besides, I've never found ongoing guilt a very useful emotion. It can simply become a form of currency, if you're not careful.

Like, payment? said Ana.

Exactly. As long as you're paying with guilt, you don't really have to change your behaviour, do you? She shrugged and smiled. It's just an idea.

And the other women?

Oh, I knew that in my body too, just didn't want to admit it at the time. But the world's a small place, such a tiny clump of consciousness really, and people started talking. My friends were furious, of course. Far angrier than I ever was.

How did that work? How did you stop being angry?

She thought of all the women Michael knew. The tightness she felt at the thought of him straying. Mikaela.

I knew him. He wasn't a bad man, really. A cad and a bounder, a real rascal, but terribly human. Even if he had women in different spots, he would never have wanted to hurt them. If he could have avoided that he would have.

I don't understand, said Ana. It's hard to imagine

being so generous when you've been hurt like that. Betrayed.

Sweetheart, it's not possible for anybody to hurt anybody else. Not ever. We only hurt ourselves. Besides, it didn't happen straightaway, the release. It was a process, of course. And ultimately vanity. I figured that resentment and bitterness made you ugly and gave you piles. She started to giggle. So I did several rituals, and after a while, all that fire, all that fury, started to subside, became smoke, and the good old phoenix rose from the ashes like a clapped-out Boeing. There you are, love. She gave her a pat on the shoulders and set the pair of scissors down on the couch. You're a picture, you know. A real peach.

Ana shook her head, could feel the hair swinging on her shoulders. Light.

And you know, Shanti continued. I learned from that, that the thing about a death – whether it's the end of a relationship, or a life – is that once it's over with, they're with you all the time, like it or not, so you may as well make peace with them.

Ana turned to look at her.

It's true. The ones you love like that, they never really go anywhere. They're in your cells, your body, the way you move. And you don't have to see them ever again, because they're part of you. It's you who gives them breath. Are you hungry?

Shanti cooked some artichokes, melted a wedge of butter, squeezed some lemon into it. How about you, flower? Did you marry that boy you were seeing here before you left?

Yes, she replied.

Going okay? asked Shanti, looking up from under the hair that had fallen across her face.

He's not happy that I'm here, she said.

Well, that makes sense. You're a beautiful woman, he probably wants you with him.

No, she said quietly. Most of the time he doesn't.

Shanti was silent.

And he's been ill. Really ill. Pneumonia.

That's no fun, said Shanti.

No, it's not. She tilted the wine glass forward and back, staring through it. I should've gone back, I suppose.

You think so? asked Shanti.

I made a vow, Shanti. In sickness and in health. I meant it.

Hmmm, said Shanti, dropping to her haunches to find some salt in the cupboard. So did he, love. It takes two to make marriage vows.

A good wife would have gone back immediately to look after him, she insisted.

Yes, said Shanti, nodding. A good wife would have shot right over there.

She bit into her cheek, while Shanti pulled the artichoke apart with her fingers.

So do you want to be good? asked Shanti. Or do you want to be true? They're not always the same thing. Here, need some salt?

She nodded, releasing a soft leaf, dipping it in the lemon butter and running it over her tongue.

Shanti reached across the table and touched her arm. You'll know what to do, flower. Trust the process. Trust yourself. Be guided by peace. Your own peace. Ever tried meditation?

Not really.

Why not give it a go, see if it works for you. It's one way of getting your mind clear. Starts off and your mind is like OK Bazaars on Christmas Eve. By the end of the meditation it's clear as Noordhoek Beach in the winter. I teach a class here on Tuesday evenings. Come along if you want to.

After supper they lifted the bicycle into the back of the bakkie and Shanti drove her home. My, it's been a long time since I've bounced up this driveway, said Shanti. The seats in the bakkie were torn, and it rattled with every hump and bump. There was a pervading smell of rotting apples.

Apples? she said to Shanti, noting a large bag on the floor.

Oh, those, nodded Shanti. For the street kids. I don't like to give them money. They just buy glue to sniff. But they're really persistent, so I try to give them fruit, when I can. Shanti glanced out the window. Ah. I see you're doing work on your wall.

Yes. Well, not me really. It's more the van der Veers' next door.

I heard Daniel was back. Send him my love.

You know him?

Yes. He and his wife – his late wife – were friends of mine.

What was she like?

Lovely. I liked her. I like Daniel too. Though he never spoke to me after she died.

Franz said she was flirtatious.

I bet he did. Shanti gave a little laugh. I never could work out with whom he was more obsessed – her, or Daniel. I don't think I've ever come across such raw sibling rivalry. From Franz's side, anyway.

What did she look like?

Like I said, she was lovely. Actually she looked a bit like you, flower. Shanti stopped her bakkie outside the kitchen door. Similar colouring.

She kissed Shanti's soft cheek and hugged her. Thank you, Shanti, she said.

It was wonderful, flower, said Shanti. Come again soon. Don't be a stranger.

She waited outside as the bakkie rattled down the road. The wine had made her feel very light, like a feather, like a bamboo whistle. She climbed the stairs and tried to light the prayer candle. But the wick had lodged itself deep into the wax, and each time she scraped it away and tried to light it, it refused the flame. Eventually she gave up, headed for her father's room, and settled herself down for the nightly serenade.

TWENTY-THREE

AND THEN THE late-night playing stopped. She tried to find him with the bansuri, the low whistle, and as a last resort, her flute.

She stood on the chair and reached to the back of the linen cupboard and pulled out the black case. She needed to take it with her, for the audition. It was the first time she'd played that instrument since her return. She would need to get to know it again. She ran through a few scales first, then some old favourites, and finally tried the piece she'd been composing on the whistle, feeling the instrument respond to her breath, to the night, a bridge between. But she played alone.

The day before she was due to leave, she woke to the sound of knocking. She reached for her watch. Only six o'clock. She wrapped a sarong around her, tying and tucking it in, rubbing her eyes, as she made her way down the stairs.

Okay, I'm coming, she said, as she reached the kitchen door. Who is it?

It's Daniel.

She opened the door, blinking into the February sun. He was carrying a small backpack.

Will you come with me for the day? he said.

Where to?

The mountains. There's something I need to show you before you go.

Now?

Now.

They walked up and behind the van der Veers' property, into the mountains.

Look, the fynbos is coming back, slowly, after the fires, he said.

It's been a year now, she said, treading between the charred remains of tree stumps, here and there small globes of green.

They do well with fire, he said. It makes them stronger, brighter, tougher.

They climbed a steep path, and he pointed towards a cave in the rock face.

I used to go there to hide when I was a kid, he said. Normally to avoid a hiding. I remember once staying there for a couple of days. It was after my friend Tom Steenkamp and I threw eggs in through the windows of his next-door neighbours' house while they were on holiday. We didn't like them. And of course, when they returned, the eggs had gone rotten. We weren't popular.

What happened?

His parents called up mine. Before the telephone conversation had even ended, I decided it was a good time to leave. To relocate. I figured the cave was a good enough spot. Angelina eventually found me. She knows all my hide-outs. Spent most of her time fishing me out of trouble, hunting me down, dragging me home.

Must have been chilly.

I think it was summer, because I don't remember being cold. At night I made a fire. I was very interested in the San at that time. Read everything I could get my hands on about them. I'd learned that they take an ember from where they lived last to light the fire at the place they will live next. So I took my father's lighter – he smoked a pipe – with me. Which did not endear me to him further, or improve my case in any way, on my return.

It was mid-afternoon before they reached the river. The faint path had disappeared some way back. She followed silently as he trod along stones and rocks, sure-footed as a leopard. He seemed to know the way, through bushes, thorns, across scrub, moss, till eventually they wandered through a small wooded area, a tunnel of trees, the boughs leaning over one another like clasped hands. At the end of the tunnel the river divided in two and he followed the left stream, till they reached a small clearing. He stopped in front of a square of earth, freshly turned, then stood to one side, so that she could see the rough wooden cross. It was simply constructed. Two short logs of Port Jackson, a nail through the middle of the one. Across the horizontal piece, carved with a knife, the word TAPIWA.

She sat on a fallen branch and stared at it. After some time, he sat down alongside her.

She was so small, he said eventually.

She nodded.

It was so fast, he said.

Aids?

I don't know. Her mother was a friend of mine in Zimbabwe. A godly woman. When she was dying she made me promise to look after Tapiwa.

Did the mother have Aids?

I don't know. It's possible. He sighed. I didn't want to know. That's the truth. I thought if I brought her to Angelina, that she'd have a chance somehow.

You did the best thing, she said. Surely you can see that?

No. If she were HIV positive, if I'd had her tested, maybe I could have done something for her.

No, she said. If she were HIV positive, you would always have been fighting the clock. You did the best you could. And you loved her. Anyone could see that, Daniel. She knew that. That's what counts.

He stared ahead, pensive, while the river splashed on. Then leaned forward and lifted a few strands of hair that had fallen across her face.

Come, he said. We should go if we want to get back before dark.

TWENTY-FOUR

To reach Paris she had to connect in Johannesburg. For the long-haul flight she had an aisle seat. Two people to her left. Put on her glasses and sank into a book before anybody around her could engage. A large woman at the window now and again took out a pink tissue, lifted her glasses and wiped away tears. She kept staring at her co-passengers, looking for something, redemption through conversation. But the man alongside her, the man in the middle who looked North African – or Kenyan perhaps – stared ahead, waiting for the plane to take off.

When it finally lunged into the sky, the woman could not contain herself any longer.

I'm leaving, she said to the man.

When he didn't respond, she repeated herself, very slowly.

I'm leaving, she said. Emigrating. Em-i-gra-ting.

He nodded.

To Canada, she said, enunciating each syllable. Leaving. South Africa.

He nodded again, looked up at the air hostess as she passed.

This is a bad, bad country, she said. A bad, *bad* country.

The man did not respond.

My daughter-in-law owns a security company in Pretoria, she said. You know, se-cu-ri-ty? And you can't believe the crime, hey.

When he didn't respond she must have felt she should justify herself further.

I'm a nurse, you know. Hospital? Joburg Gen. Joburg? And boy, have I seen them coming in. I'm not a racist. Really, I believe everybody has a right to live in peace and quiet. But it doesn't seem everybody feels the same way. Trust me, she said, shaking her head, this is a bad, *bad* country. She took out a piece of melting chocolate from her trousers, and starting sucking on it, licking her fingers. After dinner, she took a sleeping pill, stretched out as much as she could, covered her face with the airline eye-mask, and, looking like the lone ranger, started to snore.

In the covers of her book she felt she had escaped. She dropped it into her lap, and smiled sympathetically at the dark-skinned man, who shrugged and smiled back.

Where are you from? he asked. He had a strong accent, but she couldn't place it. Beautiful cheekbones and nose, soft brown skin.

Cape Town. You?

Ethiopia, he answered. But I've been living in Swaziland with my wife and three children for ten years. And what do you do? he queried further.

A pause. I've been making a garden. She wondered how it would sound out loud.

He looked amused. Is that your usual line of work?

I'm . . . I'm between lives. *A quarter tone*, she thought.

He smiled and nodded.

And you? she asked, to be polite.

I'm a surgeon, he answered. Off to Paris for a conference.

Ah. A break from the bad, *bad* country.

He smiled again, took up his newspaper, and disappeared.

TWENTY-FIVE

THE PLANE APPROACHED Paris as the morning light broke, the left wing tipping upwards as it sped over dark green fields, odd patches of snow, the occasional red roof, and prepared to land. She tilted her head and leaned against the side of the window, blinking. Every joint felt crystalline, eyes gritty. And yet, it was always the same, this sense of relief as she drew nearer.

Spat out into the airport, processed, stamped and documented, she found the queue for train tickets. An icy breeze was gusting in from the automatic doors to the trains. She buttoned up her jacket, then, clutching the leather bag in one hand, her flute case in the other, and finally the ticket, she swung herself into the carriage. The train, punctual as ever, sped past the graffiti, the concrete slabs, walls and tunnels, an old refrain. She jumped off at the Jardin du Luxembourg, and shivered, deciding to walk the short distance to the hotel to warm up.

Her audition at the Sorbonne was the following day at eleven, so she had some time to adjust. Café owners, crisp and starched, were opening up, reinstating the upturned chairs. Here and there people walked dogs. Occasionally someone shouted. In the distance she could see the road-cleaning machine, spraying the gutters with water, to clean up the dog urine and excrement. Finally she found it, Hôtel de l'Espoir. The same woman, with the same electric-blue eyeshadow rose from the reception desk to greet her. She could tell she did not recognise her. Not without Michael. *Bonjour, madame.*

The same blue bedspread and towels. White tiles in the bathroom. The *bienvenue* chocolate on the pillowcase. She took off her jacket and dropped it on the chair. Just then, the telephone rang.

Ana? Oh, good, you're there. It was Michael, from Moscow.

Did you think I wouldn't be? she answered.

I can't be sure these days, he replied. Good luck for tomorrow. Gotta fly.

At ten thirty the next day she walked up boulevard St Michel into the Place de la Sorbonne, a square full of restaurants, coffee shops, bookshops and bars, just to the one side of the university. With her free hand, she checked her watch; she was half an hour early for her audition. She considered settling into one of the red bucket chairs at the *Tabac* and ordering an espresso, then decided against it. She would rather find the exact room where her audition was to take place. In her other hand, slightly clammy, she clutched the flute case. So here she was again. About to be tried and tested. Putting herself out there, allowing someone else to decide her worth. Although this was slightly different, she conceded. She'd had this conversation with herself a thousand times already. All she really had to do was show she had potential. She was not applying for a job. She was applying to be good enough to give *them* money.

She had walked through parts of the Sorbonne before.

The frescoes, cold and beautiful on the plaster walls. The corridors that echo with history. It seemed hard to believe that she was actually here. Only a few days before she had been digging troughs and packing rocks. Girl from South Africa, about to be tested.

Scraps of paper scrambled for space on a large cork board. Accommodation notices. Part-time jobs. The door was open to the professor's office. *Bonjour, bonjour.*

He was a small man, dressed in a black polo-neck and black pants. He put out his hand to greet her. *Enchanté.* As hers flew up to meet his, she was suddenly aware of the rough skin on her palms, the callouses and the torn fingernails. She was supposed to be a classical musician. She could hardly explain that she had been mixing cement.

With one hand on her back, the other carrying a black briefcase, he guided her down some passages, into a room, comfortably heated. Even so, she shivered.

English? he asked.

She nodded.

From his briefcase he took a thin notebook and a sheaf of paper.

Some theory, he said, and a bit of harmony and counterpoint. Call me when you have finished. Then we can do the aural test and you can play for me.

She nodded, put on her glasses, then sat down at the dark wooden table. She did not find the questions too difficult. Somewhere between Mr Trimble, the start of her studies and the musical subtitles of her life with Sam she felt she could decipher most of the answers.

So what do you think, Sam? she thought, standing up when she had finished.

She knocked once again on the professor's door,

handed him her paper, then allowed him to guide her to a practice room with a desk and piano.

D'accord, he said. Some scales. C major.

She took a breath and played each note as evenly as possible. He requested a few more. Then handed her some sight-reading. She arranged it on the music stand. Looked in her handbag for the small red case, snapped it open then realised she was already wearing her glasses. She hated sight-reading more than anything.

She made two mistakes almost immediately. Could feel them reverberating through the halls. As though the people in the painted frescoes were shouting *wrong notes!*

He then asked her if she knew Poulenc's sonata for flute and piano. She nodded. Lifted the flute to her mouth again, and played. Before she finished, he motioned her to stop. She held the flute some distance from her mouth, her eyes waiting for his next instruction.

Now, *madame*, play something you love, he said. Something you love, that you know from inside.

She thought a while.

Are you sure? she said. What if it's not, strictly, classical?

It's okay, he said, with a wave of the hand. What I care about is that it is something for which you feel some fire.

She stared at him, trying to understand this challenge. Was it a trick? It was certainly a risk. It was also very far from what she expected in this place of learning. Play what she loved? She could not help but think back to her other world, to the nights of music in her father's bedroom in the dark. The nights that smelled of the sea. She looked up at him one last time. Yes, he meant it, this professor with the delicate hands and the black eyes.

All right, she said, tipping her head in acquiescence. And she took a breath and played. With her chapped fingers and chipped nails, she played the composition she had been developing all this time. In the first few notes she faltered. Then within a few bars, she had lost all sense of time and place. *To do something and forget the time*, her father would say. *Then you are lucky.* Soon the professor, the university and even Poulenc were growing very small. The memory of failed interviews in London, her own life there, its longing and its displacement all fading and shrinking. Lilliputians in toy houses, against the backdrop of mountain, sea and sun, the smell of dust and rain, her heart a drumbeat in her chest.

At the end of it, the professor gave a curt nod, before standing up behind the desk and saying *Merci*. He would let her know as soon as bureaucracy would allow, hopefully before she left. When she explained that she was in Paris only for a further few days, he shrugged and sighed. Then scribbled down the name of her hotel, before she left the building.

She stood for several minutes under the shower, her face turned upward, feeling the water running, splashing warm on her mouth, over her tongue, her eyelids. Through her hair it flowed, into the hollows of her cheeks, collarbones, dividing into rivulets between her breasts and shoulder blades. As she rubbed soap over her body, she felt the renewed firmness of flesh that had returned to her hips, her belly, a new fullness in her torso. And all around her, the rhythm of water. Drops beating and breaking on her skin, the floor, thud, thud, thud, again and again, warm and fluid as a dream.

On her last morning there, as she passed the reception desk, the woman with the blue lizard eyes handed her an envelope. *Pour vous, madame.* She did not open it then. Walked up boulevard St Michel to the Jardin du Luxembourg, to the Fontaine de Médicis. She settled herself into one of the chairs alongside the grotto and shivered. The white winter sun cut the morning like paper, and in that cold light the lovers seemed paler, more vulnerable than ever against the dark and brooding Polyphemus. She wrapped her jacket around herself and listened to the sound of the wind. Eerie. She opened her eyes and noticed that the fountain was switched off for the winter. Then she took out the envelope from her bag. She had already seen the Sorbonne postmark, icon of knowledge, on the back. Knew where it was from before she tore it open.

The letter thanked her for coming for the audition and served as a preliminary invitation to enrol in their Music and Musicology Programme. It also mentioned that some funding opportunities were available for foreign students should she require financial assistance. It confirmed that an official letter, together with the necessary application forms, would be posted to her residential address in the coming weeks.

She stared up again at the statue, at the jealous Polyphemus, about to throw the fatal rock at the rival Acis. What secrets, what dark memories do you keep in your stone? She looked down at her hands, the hands that had helped to build a wall, still holding the letter. And then suddenly, she knew his Flaubertian reply. Imagined the enormous bronze statue leaning one degree closer and whispering: *Mais Polyphème, c'est toi.* When she closed her eyes to think, she heard children's laughter in the wind. Tapiwa. And in her mind's eye saw the riverbank in the mountains where the ashes of her once warm little body had been returned to the earth.

After some time, she left the Jardin du Luxembourg. She had the afternoon free till she would have to make her way to the airport to catch the plane back to Johannesburg, then Cape Town. She walked first up the cobbled street, along rue Soufflot to St-Etienne-du-Mont, where she lit a candle, then knelt on the red velvet cushion. Prayer to Ste Geneviève.

Thank you.

Then she wandered down to the river, just across from Notre Dame, to rue de la Bûcherie, to Shakespeare and Company. Michael had taken her there before. Told her about how in the fifties, after the Second World War, it had become synonymous with literary gatherings, particularly amongst ex-pats. They had visited there, the two of them, Michael pointing out the uneven bookshelves, the chaotic filing. Now, on her own, she scanned the rows of new books, old books, philosophy books amongst the architecture journals, English, French, all leaning towards her like old friends eager to gossip. She heard the rustle of feet behind her and stifled a gasp. It would take time before the mugging left her completely.

Pardon, she said, containing the fright.

A slender old man with white hair and a wispy voice stood up and greeted her.

You can stay here, he said. Did you know that? You can stay here.

She swung round to see if he were addressing someone behind her, but there was nobody.

Writers, poets, can stay here, if they need to, he said. There's accommodation upstairs.

I'm not a writer, she said.

No, but you're an artist, he said. Don't argue with me.

She smiled and nodded, weaving through uneven bookcases, vaguely alphabetised.

She found a book called *The Indigenous Wisdom of Africa*. Was leafing through it when he suddenly popped up again next to her. Have you seen the gallery? he insisted, handing her a key on a large wooden key ring. Third floor, through the iron door.

It was like an invitation from C.S. Lewis. She took the key and made her way up the steep and narrow staircase, the shop unpeeling, floor by floor, like an onion, layers of life between thumbprints and footprints on every level, in every nook. Finally she reached the iron door. As she tried the key in the lock, the door swung open, a very tall man was just leaving.

Come in, he said. An American. We've been speaking about James Joyce. I'm writing a book.

He introduced his friend, who was sitting at a round table with a crocheted table cloth. Suddenly he didn't appear to be leaving anymore.

I was told there is a gallery? she enquired.

Ah, yes. Photographs. Let me show you. The tall American guided her through the labyrinthine room, velvet scatter cushions, old couches, the occasional single bed and a grubby kitchen, through to a wall where there were original photographs of Henry Miller and Anaïs Nin, Ernest Hemingway and Gertrude Stein, Ginsberg and Durrell. She recognised the owner of the bookstore in most of the pictures, younger, happier.

Writers stay here for free, said the tall American. You're supposed to help out in the shop in return, an hour a day.

And read a book daily, chipped in the other, shorter American.

Sounds lovely, she said, heading for the door.

Wait, don't go. Would you have dinner with me tonight? said the tall American as she thanked them and prepared to leave.

I have a plane to catch, she replied.

The weather had turned by the time she left the bookshop. The sky lower than she'd ever seen it in Paris before. A seasonal shift of light. Paris of Polyphemus. She ducked into a small store that sold miscellaneous tourist items, clichés-to-go. Robert Doisneau T-shirts, or caps with imprints of the Eiffel Tower, small bells with pictures of Notre Dame, and postcards of sophisticated black cats. In the corner, slightly dusty, she noticed some candles. A bright yellow one caught her eye.

Yes, she thought, lifting it and taking it to the cashier.

She walked along the river until she found some steps leading down to its banks. Wandered alongside some old boats, oil seeping into the river here and there, before stopping, kneeling down and staring at her reflection, lapping and swaying, towards her, then away. The cold stung her cheeks. She took the letter from the envelope she'd received that morning, the letter from the Sorbonne, and folded it carefully into small squares. Took her spectacles case from her bag, removed the glasses, wrapped them in some tissues and placed them in her bag. Then she fitted the folded paper inside the neat red case, and, with all the force she could muster, tossed it as far as she could into the river.

Some minutes later, a pitchfork of lightning jabbed the air, with it a crack of thunder, like a mighty rock hurled across the clouds. Then the skies broke and all the great tears of heaven fell. People in coats blurred under the weight, dipping and darting like birds. She walked back up the steps into the street, then waited. Turned her head as if to witness her footsteps effaced by the rain. See? No print of her visit. No trace of her now in the city of light. Only other people's feet flurrying for cover and a pulverised packet of Gitanes decomposing on the cobblestones. And the wind. The wind the sound of the low whistle, and crows scudding between buildings. She lifted her head and inhaled. Somewhere in the wet of oil and fumes, filtering through filaments of memory, the hint of flowers. She made her way back down the stairs and in the wash of water walked alongside the Seine and watched. Still she could make it out, that small red case bobbing in the waves. Bobbing at walking pace through the barges, through the debris, through the branches, before being swept into the swirling darkness, the words tucked inside it like some last lines of love, sucked into the rhythms of that sullen river as it surged to the sea.

TWENTY-SIX

THE FLIGHT BACK to Johannesburg gave her space. For once there was nobody in the seat alongside her, and she could curl up with her thoughts and lean against the window as the plane forged through the night. The cottage. She was making good headway with the garden, now it was time to tackle the house. She would not be able to afford to straightaway, but perhaps if she gave some music lessons, sold the motorbike and side-car. She'd like to replace the old brown counters in the kitchen. She could buy some tiles or paint her own. She would find a book and teach herself. Her mind drifted to the living room, with its old crocheted antimacassars and threadbare chairs. Those too could use new covers, sanding down. Even the workshop in the loft – it was time to put those tools and all that wood in the shed. She could sleep there instead, turn her bedroom into a storage room. That left her father's room. It's time, Sam, she thought. Time to put some of your things away. You can drink a memory dry. Till it curls up like a leaf in winter, and keeps breaking into tinier pieces. It's time to look up. That room where you slept has so much of you, so much light. I thought about making it a music room. I can make a special thing to hang my flute and my whistles on the wall. I can use the desk for composing.

As the last trolleys of drinks had rattled away, and the

lights were switched off, she drifted along with the drone of the engines. Fragments of the day she'd spent in the mountains, walking through the unknown paths of Silvermine Nature Reserve in the arms of the African sun, the remains of the fire a year ago still evident. To know the places people go to hide. Brief cameos, clips of the last few months, floated in and out, bringing their rhythm, their images, their sensations. Certain cadences started to gather together, gather form, momentum, bringing with them words, clumps of words, like rocks in a wheelbarrow, awaiting their alignment. She found a pencil, switched on the tiny night-light, and on the back of the menu started jotting. By the time the plane was ready to land in Johannesburg, she had finished it.

Silvermine walking, late summer
the sun's last streamers strewn across
the sky, where silence rises like water, like
dust, the wind, breath of earth exhaling
the sea's incense of salt and fin

This place, where
all over everywhere, between
alchemies of dying – filigrees
of fynbos and vygies, small skulls
of ash, of bone, where wisps of memory
twist and ghosts of fire still gust –
new buds are birthing, pushing
green into the rib of heaven

We walk and whisper
careful not to shout or touch, lest
we disturb some bigger force, some
greater hand that holds the torch, the river

This place, this now
this light that is both night
and day, this rust of soil
and stone, this heart
where all that is forgiven
grows again

Franz had agreed to meet her at the airport back in Cape Town. She spotted him from inside the baggage claim area, from where she hovered round the carousel clutching her flute case and waiting for her bag. Instead of the tiredness that usually hung heavy around his shoulders, he looked buoyant. Luminous. Maybe he'd gone to Shanti for a cleansing. *When pigs fly!* She grinned at the thought.

You look transformed, she said as she walked alongside the railing with her bag. I should go away more often.

No. Don't do that, he said. Here, let me help you. Give those to me. How was it?

No, it's okay, she said, handing him the leather bag. I'll carry the flute.

So? How was it? he repeated. He looked nervous as he waited for her reply.

It's good to be back, she said.

Still in love with Paris?

Always, she smiled.

He nodded, as though accepting what was coming. Did it love you back this time?

He dipped into his jeans pocket to find some money for the parking.

A little, I suppose, she smiled. Or as much as it could in a week. But you know, I think the love affair needs to stay just that. A meaningful flirtation. Otherwise where can I escape to? If I live there, I'll know all about those everyday things that ruin a relationship – how they treat their homeless, why they eat horses. Maybe if I love it from a distance, the romance will last for ever. But how are you? You look rejuvenated. Have you had a holiday? Taken a break at last?

He did not reply. The sun was hot as they walked along the tarmac looking for the Pajero.

He opened the car door and threw her leather bag in the back, turning to face her before she climbed in.

Look, Ana, you need to know, he said.

Yes?

Daniel.

What?

Daniel's gone, he said, matter-of-fact.

She stopped and faced him, her hand on the top of the door.

What do you mean? You make it sound like a cat's gone missing. Where did he go?

I don't know, Ana. One never does. Not even Angelina. He finished the last bit of the wall the day you left. Packed up and left that night.

As they climbed the last stretch of the driveway, she dug in the pouch of her leather bag for her house keys. Thanked him for the lift, said she needed to rest after her flight, then closed the car door and headed for the kitchen.

The house was strangely musty, the smell of something rotting somewhere. She unlocked the interleading door, the panelled yellowwood one she had watched her father make, *dead as a doornail*. Perhaps it was a rat. But she didn't wait to find it. She went back to the kitchen, grabbed the bag, her flute case, and took them upstairs, where she dropped them on her bed. She did not open anything, did not unpack, or shower, or rest. Instead, she kicked off her shoes, put on her takkies and ran out of the door. She walked quickly. As though each step would take her away, take her to some place, some tree or bush, somewhere she could crawl into or under. Some place where she could wait for things to stop, till she could find that space inside, cool and quiet, where things go to die.

At last she reached the river, to the soft patch of grass, soft like wheat, slightly flattened from her visits. She tossed her takkies into a nearby bush and lay back, face up to the sky. Watched the clouds, forming, moving, dissolving. Filling, emptying. Wondered if there was anything quite as empty as the sky.

After most of the day had passed, she heard the footfall of someone coming. It crossed her mind that it could be an intruder, or Franz. But she didn't move, or care. Turned her head and watched the figure in the distance, swaying like a song in the late afternoon. Angelina. The older woman seemed to know where to find her, knew where she had run to hide, where she was lying, jeans rolled up, one foot swinging in the water. She sat down alongside her, with a big heave and a sigh.

They sat in silence, till she said, Look, Angelina, the water is golden. Tannins in the water. Like tea.

Angelina took her hand, covered it with both of hers.

Where did he go? Ana asked.

I don't know, said Angelina, shrugging her large shoulders. He never say. His work was finished here. The baby died.

Ana nodded.

Also he know you are *nkosikazi*, married woman. And he know that *Nkosaan* Franz like you too much. He don't want same story like before.

She thinks of the book of photographs on Franz's coffee table at the big house. The woman blown by the wind alongside a canal in Venice, eating a plum.

But I am not that woman.

No, you are not that woman. But you look little bit like her. First time I see you, I get fright, remember? That day you come to the house from next door? I think you must be sister or something.

The river threw off sparks of water here and there, catching the light then dying.

What will happen? Ana asked.

The older woman shrugged again. That is another story. Maybe it is yours, I don't know. Then with a sigh, Angelina hoisted herself up onto her feet.

And you know, she said, dusting off her hands, when you find that story – that one that is yours – then you will know you are home.

She walked back to the house. Ran a bath. So much to rinse away. So much that she had ignored the familiar tugging in her lower, slightly distended belly. When she rose from the water a line of blood ran like a tear to her foot.

Back downstairs she poured herself a glass of wine, then sat at the kitchen table. All around the cottage the wind. She got up and switched on the radio. Nina Simone, *You Took My Teeth*. She inhaled the wine, then took a deep mouthful. It would be quiet from now on. No more sound of banging at the wall. No more motorbike engine revving. She stood up again and turned the radio up a little more. The odour was pervasive. She checked the fridge, but there was nothing rotting there, then pushed open the window, noticing it was cracked and chipped in one corner. Suddenly the smell was stronger. She opened the back door onto the garden she had been working in. The cluster of giant sunflowers were settling in around the sundial. But there was something else. In the corner next to the mermaid, the wheelbarrow Daniel had used to fetch rocks had been filled with soil and seedlings. She dropped down close and peered at them, it looked as though the first tight buds of some Barberton daisies were getting ready to flower. At the foot of the wheelbarrow were two empty bags of chicken manure. That explained the odour. The mermaid stared back at her with her limpid eyes, her hands outstretched. Around her neck, on a piece of string, hung a small hand-painted whistle, made from what looked like river reed. She lifted it over the statue's head and examined it, raised it to her mouth and blew into it, surprised at the purity of its pitch.

She suddenly remembered something, and darted inside the house, returning with the yellow candle she'd found in Paris and some matches. She balanced it on the statue's grainy fingers and lit the wick, watching the flame burn yellow, rise and fall. Thought about what he'd told her about the nomadic San. *An ember from where they lived last to light the fire at the place they will live next.*

It was growing dark when she returned indoors after watering the seedlings. The smell of chicken manure was diluted. She placed the candle in the centre of the kitchen table, watching its flame add dimension to the night.

Would he return? She could not know.

For a time, who knows how long, late at night she may tilt her head and listen. For a time. She may run through the constellation of decisions, the sky of absences that had brought her to this place. Back, yet beginning. Familiar, yet new. She may wonder how it may have been had he stayed. How the tide of her life may have turned. For a time. And then, maybe one day, yet another season will change. Another leaf will grow, another fall. And somewhere in the silence of herself, she will accept it.

Sometimes there are no words. The river takes them to the sea.

She felt the shiver of a draft streaming through the chipped kitchen window. Turned to look at it. She remembered the handyman who had replaced the pane in her father's workshop. The putty, the turps, the panel pins. *Everything's easy when you know how, ma'am.* She'd go to the hardware shop and get the materials. She'd give it a try.

Eventually she takes the candle with her upstairs. By its light she climbs into her father's bed, turns to watch it flicker, before blowing it out. As she sinks into the pillowy arms of sleep, in her mind's eye, she can still see the imprint of the candle burning. With every rise and fall of breath, she sees it, feels it. Warm as the sun. Yellow as a field of sunflowers. Till silhouettes start to form, twist free from the liquid blue of the flame. Ghosts of fire shaking loose their shoulders and their hair. Ghosts and shadows, fluid, swaying, to the distant sound of drums, to the rhythms of the past, to the slow beat of tomorrow.

GLOSSARY

aangename kennis (Afrikaans) – pleased to meet you

aikhona (Zulu) – no / no way

à la chambre (French) – room service

bergie (Afrikaans) – vagrant

bienvenue (French) – welcome

cinquième (French) – fifth, here referring to a specific district

daai bliksem (Afrikaans) – that rogue

église (French) – church

eish (Zulu) – untranslatable, but something like wow / my goodness / no!

enchanté (French) – enchanted / pleased to meet you

fynbos (Afrikaans) – fine-leafed plant indigenous to South Africa

haaibo (Zulu) – oh my goodness

hawu (Zulu) – gosh, my goodness

mais Polyphème, c'est toi (French) – but you are Polyphemus

nee, dankie (Afrikaans) – no thank you

nkosaan (Zulu) – boss

nkosana (Zulu) – younger boss / little brother

Nkosi Sikele iAfrica (Xhosa / national anthem of South Africa) – *God Bless Africa*

nou goed dan (Afrikaans) – not directly translatable, but something like No, good / Okay then phelile (Zulu) – finished / over

pour vous, madame (French) – for you, madam

ravissante (French) – ravishing / gorgeous

stoep (Afrikaans) – verandah / porch

suka (Zulu)– come off it / mind out the way

toyi-toyi – protest dance

tula baba, tula sana – Zulu / Xhosa lullaby, hush baby

vignes (French) – vines

vygies (Afrikaans) – succulent plant indigenous to South
    Africa

volledig (Afrikaans) – complete

ACKNOWLEDGEMENTS

The quotation at the start of the book is from 'History is the Home Address', from the book of the same name, by Mongane Wally Serote, published by Kwela, 2004.

The second quotation is from the poem 'Land in Sight' by Anne Michaels from her volume *Skin Divers*, published by Bloomsbury in 1999.

Information about ICTs in Africa is available from, amongst other sources, the United Nations Economic Commission for Africa, www.uneca.org/aisi.

I am grateful to those involved with the publication of this book, particularly Briony Everroad and Geoff Mulligan. Thanks also to the librarians at UCT for information on the Soweto riots. To Susan Levine for her knowledge about the toyi-toyi. And to Conrad Ketterer, Roger Lucey, Bill Robson, Viola Lengner, Kobus Conradie, Béatrice Roudet, André Brink and Karina Dorn, Duduzile Makhathini, Lisa Glanz, Sue Whiley, Alta Fölscher, Bob Michaelson, and Glen Bresler.

Special thanks to Robbie and Sen Lessem.

SUSAN MANN

One Tongue Singing

Camille Pascal, a young, unmarried French nurse comes to South Africa with her father and her small daughter, Zara, during the closing years of the apartheid regime. The family settles amongst a wine-growing community in the Western Cape where they become involved in the lives of victims of the System. Interwoven with Camille's story is that of Jake Coleman, a painter with an international reputation, a deep-seated fear of failure, and a complicated private life. It is in the exclusive Jake Coleman School of Art that Zara, now a talented artist in her late teens, decides to enrol. She is a feral, troubled girl, obsessed with scenes of violence, and quite unlike anything Jake has encountered. *One Tongue Singing* explores some of the different faces of power, both in the ways it operates between individuals and in societies. It is written with economy, humanity and a hard brilliance, and it announces a distinctive new voice from South Africa.

'Sensitive and sharp and charged with authentic passion, this is a book that sings in a tongue of liquid fire. Behind its intricate play of light and darkness lies an affirmation that ultimately life is worth living. First novels rarely come better'
André Brink

'A superbly crafted novel, in terms of language, characterisation and plot, *One Tongue Singing* is not a love story, but a story of choice and consequence and the nature of the lives that we live'
Herald

'Strong on characterisation, *One Tongue Singing* is an incisive and emotive reminder that power in human relationships always manages to transcend colour, gender, wealth or class'
Guardian

VINTAGE BOOKS
London

www.vintage-books.co.uk